Return

To

Baskerville

First edition published in 2025
© Copyright 2025
Allison Osborne

The right of Allison Osborne to be identified as the author of this work has been asserted by her in accordance with the Copyright, Designs and Patents Act 1998.

All rights reserved. No reproduction, copy or transmission of this publication may be made without express prior written permission. No paragraph of this publication may be reproduced, copied or transmitted except with express prior written permission or in accordance with the provisions of the Copyright Act 1956 (as amended). Any person who commits any unauthorised act in relation to this publication may be liable to criminal prosecution and civil claims for damage.

All characters appearing in this work are fictitious. Any resemblance to real persons, living or dead, is purely coincidental. The opinions expressed herein are those of the author and not of Orange Pip Books.

ePub ISBN 978-1-80424-672-6
PDF ISBN 978-1-80424-673-3
Paperback ISBN 978-1-80424-674-0

Published by Orange Pip Books
335 Princess Park Manor, Royal Drive,
London, N11 3GX
www.orangepipbooks.com

Holmes & Co. Mysteries

Collection one
The Introduction of Holmes & Co
A Study in Victory Red
The Circle Code Conundrum
The Impossible Murderer
The Happy Family Facade
The Red Rover Society
The Detective's Nemesis

Collection Two
The Adventures of Holmes & Co
The Hidden Case
The Missing Two
The American Visitors
The Dismantled Minds
The French Translator
Return to Baskerville

The past and the present are within the field of my inquiry, but what a man may do in the future is a hard question to answer.

-Sherlock Holmes, *The Hound of the Baskervilles*

Chapter I

Mr. Franklin Dearborn

Irene Holmes stared at the blank stationary in front of her as she sat at her desk near the window overlooking Baker Street. She'd been trying to write a letter to her father for the past week, but never made it further than 'Hello', which she always crossed out to think of a better greeting.

Miss Hudson offered to mail the letter every day. Irene wasn't sure if she was ready to send it even if she did finish it.

A passing bus outside caught her attention. She stared out the window for another half hour, then spent another ten minutes or so fiddling with her short hair, twirling the dark strands into a few pin curls, still not quite used to its length since getting it cut a few weeks ago.

It wasn't until much later that she finally sighed and pushed away from the desk.

Perhaps Miss Hudson could offer some encouragement. Or a distraction.

Normally she'd turn to her dear friend for such a thing, but Joe had gone round to the pub with Eddy. Or had he gone to the shops with Sarah? Irene paused and listened, but didn't hear him upstairs in his room. He'd definitely left 221b for... somewhere.

So, Miss Hudson it was.

Irene wandered down the long staircase to the first floor flat and rapped on the door. She didn't wait for an answer before entering her landlady's sitting room. The lady in question sat on a worn out dark green chair. She had a few sections of quilt on her lap and a needle in one hand.

"Hello, Love," she greeted, smiling, Scottish brogue lilting every word. "What brings you down?"

"I was wondering if you required help with anything?"

Miss Hudson raised a brow. "You're offering your help?"

"Yes."

"Willingly?"

"Yes."

"What did you break?"

Irene scoffed. "Nothing, of course. Can't I just offer help with no other motivation?"

The older woman eyed her, then nodded to her quilt. "I have nothing to do but this until tonight's tea. You are more than welcome to grab a square."

Irene did her best to hide her expression of disgust, but then she opened her mouth. "I would rather pluck off my own fingernails and study them under a microscope, Miss Hudson."

She huffed. "Well, go on and do that then!"

Irene sighed and trudged back upstairs, staring at her newly painted fingernails. They shone bright red in the overhead lights. Although the polish still felt a bit heavy on her nails, a part of her did enjoy how feminine it made her sometimes gnarled fingers – even if it did chip easily. And while pulling off a red fingernail would create some activity for her, she forwent that task and dragged out the box of Christmas decor from the closet in her bedroom. The first of December was tomorrow, and a decorated flat seemed to put everyone in a good mood.

So, why not start early?

It was certainly better than forcing herself to write a letter she was never going to send anyway.

* * * * *

Half an hour later, Christmas had vomited all over 221b. A paper chain was twice wrapped around Irene's neck and ornaments hung from every finger. Nothing was hung, as she debated where to place everything this year; she wanted to make it perfect. Stumbling over yet another angel Miss Hudson kept giving her, she neared her desk, and the start of the paper chain, dutifully ignoring the still open letter next to the stack of envelopes. Irene stood on the chair to hang the loop on the hook that she'd left up since last year when a knock came from the front door.

Strong. Purposeful.

A client.

She leapt from the chair, scooping the dangling chain as she went. She dropped the ornaments gingerly back into the box. Scrambling out of the paper chains, she shoved everything into her bedroom and shut the door just in time for Miss Hudson to give a small rap on the flat's door. Irene smoothed her trousers and finger combed her hair, then moved a blanket from her chair to Joe's.

"Come in."

Miss Hudson opened the door and shuffled in. The man that entered behind her was paunchy, rotund and sweaty, despite the cooler temperature outside. His face was clean-shaven, however, and his teeth white. His clothes, at first glance, were of the expensive kind, despite being all drab shades of brown.

This man had money. And was willing to part with it, if his wide eyes and toothy, excited grin was anything to go by.

"Irene Holmes!" He pushed past Miss Hudson and held out his hand to her.

She recoiled at his eagerness and shook her head. "I do not shake hands."

"Oh *please?* It is truly an honour to meet you!"

Swallowing another grimace, she grasped the man's surprisingly dry hand. He nearly shook her arm off. Once she finally retrieved her hand back, she gestured to the couch.

Miss Hudson still stood in the doorway, a white brow arched. Irene gave her a curt nod and she left to make the tea.

Now sat, the man gazed around the flat as if it were a museum.

"My partner, Dr—"

"Watson, yes," the man cut her off, "your trusty colleague. Is he not in?"

Irene turned to the fire, grabbing the poker to stoke the flame. "He is out at the moment."

"Oh, what a shame. At least you're here though!"

She kept the poker with her as she sat in her chair. While this man didn't seem inherently dangerous, he was exceptionally excited to meet her and to be in her flat. Irene didn't trust anyone that excited about anything.

"How can I help you Mr…"

"Franklin Dearborn." He shifted on the couch, eager to speak. "Oh, Miss Holmes, I have made the purchase of the century! You see, I am somewhat of a Sherlock Holmes enthusiast, and when this particular item came to market, I could not help myself."

Irene stiffened. Items of her father's were being sold? What did they have? What were people doing with her father's belongings? What could someone out there possibly have that she didn't?

This man spoke about his admiration for her father as if he was some film star or famous public figure.

"What item," she bit out.

"Baskerville Hall." Franklin paused for some type of dramatic effect but it only made Irene more cross.

"A house? A house that didn't even belong to Sherlock Holmes?"

"It's the most famous house in the world! The story of Sherlock Holmes and the great hound is the best story I have ever read, and when I saw that one could purchase *the* estate?

Well, I offered what the man wanted, and more, to ensure I got it."

Irene stared, her lip twitching in both disgust and confusion.

"So why come to me? Sherlock Holmes solved whatever mysteries were there at the house ages ago."

"True, Miss Holmes." This was the third time he'd used her name in all of five minutes and Irene was rather annoyed. The man continued though, and she knew he would call her name several times more. "The house seems safe, but I would still like it checked. I know your father disproved the giant hound theory, but the lands are still magical. There may still be a creature out there."

Irene stared at him. "A magical creature? If you are such a fanatic of Sherlock Holmes, then you'd know he never dealt with magic and fantasy."

"Yes, yes, Miss Holmes. Of course." Dearborn rooted around in his bag and pulled out a cheque. "I am prepared to pay a hefty sum. And this is only half of what I would offer. Come to Baskerville and you'll get the other half."

Irene stared at the cheque, the numbers sinking in. Fifteen hundred pounds shone up at her like a barrel of treasure. Between this money and the funds they received a few weeks ago from a French gangster, they'd have enough for an entire *building*, let alone an office space.

She looked at him again, but held tight to the cheque. "I do not understand. What are we there to do?"

He gestured wildly. "Walk around! Take in the place! See if there is anything that I should be concerned about."

Though the job sounded easy enough, she was wary. It sounded too good to be true. And yet, this very excitable man simply looked like he wanted to be in her presence. A train ride, a walk around an old estate, and a line or two quoting Father to assure this man the hall was hound-free was no skin off her nose.

She glanced at the cheque again and knew that, even if the trip ended up being slightly more of a challenge, this amount of money would be worth it.

She looked at Dearborn who was practically falling off the sofa as he leaned forward waiting for her answer. "Dr. Watson and I will come to Baskerville Estate."

"Ah! What wonderful news, Miss Holmes! Tonight then!"

"Tonight?" Irene kept a grasp on the cheque as she raised a brow. "The train ride is three hours at least."

The man nodded vigorously, wispy hair floating about. "Yes, and if you take the three-fifteen, it should get you there right on time."

"On time for what?"

"The evening!"

"If we are simply walking around the estate, why is there a very specific time?"

Dearborn's demeanour shifted and he wrung his hands, askance, and chuckled nervously. "I am still hiring staff and all of them are here today. I assume you'd want to interview everyone, right? This is the only day I could collect everyone before I officially move in. Plus, I have a friend or two coming for the evening whom I'd love for you to meet as well, as they will be frequently staying in the estate. Just to be sure they are to be trusted."

"You do not trust your friends?"

"Oh, I do, but I've recently come into these funds, and friendships change when there is money involved."

An audience and staff to interview changed the task completely. She had no desire to schmooze with people who may also have an affinity for her father and wanted to talk her ear off.

However, the cheque burned a hole through her fingers as the amount was truly exorbitant. She glanced at Joe's empty chair, trying to imagine what his answer would be. A quick walk around, a few handshakes, and some smiles for practically a year's salary? He would be in favour, she was sure. He would tug her aside and convince her this was an easy job. Between the money, the fun train ride, and a stroll around a large, spooky estate, just to tell a man there is nothing to be feared, there was no real reason to say no.

After all, what could go wrong?

She looked back at the man, at the edge of the sofa again, sweat drops on his forehead. "Dr. Watson and I will be there tonight. If you make this cheque three-quarters up front."

He grinned at her, then yanked his cheque book out. They traded papers and he ripped up the smaller amount.

"Bless you, Miss Holmes. You will not regret this visit. I will see you tonight!"

He stood and scurried around the couch, but paused at the door. Dearborn looked around the flat – from the fireplace to the windows and back to the door – giddy as anything, as if he were standing in the Queen's quarters at Buckingham Palace. He gave her a final nod before finally leaving.

As soon as the front door of 221 shut, Irene shouted, "Miss Hudson! Miss Hudson, come here!"

The older woman took a donkey's age to get up the stairs but finally huffed and puffed into the flat. "What is it?"

Irene held out the cheque. "Please cash this for us while we are away. Also, where is Joe?"

The landlady took the cheque and gasped. "Oh, Irene. What did he ask of you?"

"To investigate Baskerville, simple as that. Now, where is Joe?"

"Out to lunch with Edward at Mac's fish shop. Did you forget?"

Irene started toward the door. "Of course not, just keeping your memory sharp!"

Miss Hudson squeezed past her as she tugged her boots on. "Be careful at Baskerville. Your father had nothing good to say about that place."

Irene waved her off and ignored the small pang of guilt as she thought about the letter she *should* be writing to Father. "That was a long time ago. And for the sum that man is paying us, I will tell him whatever he wants to hear. Now, I must find Joe!"

Chapter II

A Train Ride to Baskerville

Doctor Joe Watson glanced across the street yet again as the poster for the newest Don Radcliffe film flashed in the sunlight.

"Quit looking at that." DI Lestrade craned his neck to glean the same poster. "You've been glaring at it since we sat down."

The men were enjoying a rare lunch together. While they were good friends, it wasn't often they had a chance to visit with one another outside of the cases they worked on.

"You want to tell me why you're still so annoyed at that man?" Lestrade asked. "I haven't heard Irene mention his name at all. She's probably forgotten it, in fact."

Joe sighed and thought of Irene's reveal to him a few weeks prior. "She spent the night with him once the case was finished. Or rather, the evening with him."

Lestrade paused mid sip of his beer. "Spent the evening as in…"

Joe nodded.

"What's troubling you about that? Did he hurt her?" Lestrade didn't sound nearly as worried as Joe expected him to. Perhaps he knew? Or perhaps he trusted Irene to make her own decisions…

Joe bit back another sigh. "He didn't hurt her, no. She said she enjoyed herself."

The DI finished his beer. "And that's what you don't like."

Joe shrugged. "I know I don't like the idea that she was with him. Would he listen to what she wants? She's very particular."

Lestrade pursed his lips but his eyes danced with amusement. "Do you not like the idea because you don't want her to get hurt, or – and forgive me if this is overstepping – because you wish it was you that was with her instead?"

Ice filled Joe's veins. He chased it away with a sip of his own beer. That was a bold assumption of Lestrade, but nothing he hadn't considered himself. The truth was: he had no idea why he was angry, and had no desire to search his feelings and find out, lest there be… desire.

Lestrade leaned forward. "If you're taking this long to answer, then I think you already know."

"Feelings are complicated."

The DI chuckled. "I almost miss the war, when all you felt was scared and romance didn't matter."

"Simpler times, eh?"

Frantic movement came from the window next to them. Irene stood on the other side of the glass waving her hands, big grin on her face. She said something Joe couldn't hear.

He sighed. "Oh dear."

"What?"

"Irene found us."

Joe watched through the window as she scurried down and flung the pub door open. Her hair, which she'd cut to her shoulders a few weeks ago, bounced as she hurried toward them. She plunked down in the seat next to Lestrade and scooted closer to him, the chair screeching on the wood floor.

"To what do we owe this pleasure," the DI laughed.

Irene shoved a few of his chips in her mouth. "We have an invitation."

"We do?" Lestrade slid the plate away from her.

"Not you. Joe and I." She switched from Lestrade's plate to Joe's. He let her eat as clearly she was excited and prone to bite his hand if interrupted.

"To where?" he asked, offering his untouched glass of water.

"Baskerville Hall." She took a big swig of water. "In Dartmoor."

"Baskerville," Lestrade repeated. "As in… the hound?"

Irene rolled her eyes. "There was never a hound."

She swallowed her mouthful of food and wiped her mouth before starting in on the tale of Mr Dearborn and the sum he'd handed over for a simple task of investigating an empty estate.

Lestrade let out a whistle. "For that amount, I'd do jumping jacks in his parlour if he asked me to."

"That's odd, Eddy."

The DI went to argue but Joe cut him off. "I suppose if the man has enough money to purchase the estate, this is a drop in the bucket to him. I assume you told Mr. Dearborn that we accept his offer?"

"Of course."

Lestrade snorted and tipped his beer glass back, catching the last few drops. "Clearly I am in the wrong profession. A few handshakes and assurance the place isn't full of ghosts or a deadly hound for that amount of money is ridiculous."

"Ridiculously wonderful," Irene interjected. "Now, let's go. We must catch the train. I will be waiting by the auto down the street."

As quick as she came in, she flew out of the pub and disappeared.

Lestrade waved for the bill as Joe finished of the last of his chips.

Irene had parked the 34' Vauxhall in front of Lestrade's Wolseley, but instead of leaning against it, or waiting in the driver's seat as Joe expected, she stood at a shop window. The two men joined her as she gazed upon a pair of earrings. The gold dropped down and encrusted a green pearl.

"Those would match my green dancing dress," Irene said.

"They would."

They were, in fact, the same green as the dress Joe had purchased for her last Christmas, almost as if the jeweller made them specially for her.

"Are you finally turning into a proper lady?" Lestrade teased.

"Perhaps I am." She gave one final poke at the glass as if saving the image in her mind. Joe made a mental note too, in case he ran out of ideas to get her this Christmas. Jewellery was an intimate gift, but Irene wouldn't think too deep into the implication of something like that.

"Be careful at Baskerville," Lestrade said as she dug the keys from her bag.

She rolled her eyes. "This is hardly a case like that."

"I know. But if I don't say it and something happens, I will take the blame."

"The bad guys are to blame, Eddy. Not you. But we will be careful. We always are."

Irene climbed into the Vauxhall and shut the door, waiting for Joe.

Lestrade stuck his hand out. "To you, I say the same. Be careful."

"Thank you. We will." Joe shook the man's hand.

* * * * *

Within a few hours, Joe and Irene sat across from one another on a train headed to Dartmoor. Irene couldn't sit still. A mere ten minutes into the journey, she shook her head and stood.

"I changed my mind. I cannot sit this way. I must face forward with the train."

Joe chuckled, expecting her change of heart, and scooped up his bag.

Irene settled into the seat. "Much better."

Joe pulled a book from his bag and held it out to her. "Your uncle's original story. I brought it in case we need to refer to it. You're more than welcome to read through it if you want."

She glanced at the copy of *The Hound of the Baskervilles* quickly before looking back out the window. "You read it and retain the knowledge, then I only have to ask you about something and you can recite it to me."

They had been slowly working through the Great Detective's stories. Mostly the ones that were mystery-heavy and kept the personal and private lives of her father and uncle to a minimum. Which meant they'd only gotten around to reading four. Joe always read them out loud. He didn't know if hearing his voice helped her disassociate the stories from her family, or because his reading soothed her, like it always had.

He didn't push the issue; he simply placed the book back in his bag. He'd read the story a few times – most recently a few weeks ago – so now it was just a weight to carry around.

He dug out another book; one he knew she'd read. She eyed the title – *The Hobbit* – then shifted in her seat, wrapping her arms around herself.

"I enjoy it better when you read it to me."

Joe swallowed a sigh. Clearly his friend was agitated, or perhaps it was a touch of nerves returning to a place her father had been. Regardless, he set the book beside her and took yet another novel from his bag to start reading himself.

* * * * *

An automobile awaited them at the Dartmoor train station, and they were whisked away to Baskerville Hall. The grounds were expansive, with the estate right in the middle, looming over the browning lawn. The building itself was a tall three-story square building, with flat walls separated into three spires.

Light fog had settled in the dips of the hills and moved into the deep forest at the back of the property. It was eery and spooky and sent a chill down Joe's spine. A small part of him, though, was thrilled to be at a location of such a famous story.

The driver dropped them at the front steps and sped away as if chased.

Joe rang the bell of the front door and within a few seconds a man in a stiff suit opened it. He had to be well over six feet tall, and almost as wide. He grunted a greeting and stepped aside, welcoming them in. Irene gave the man a once over, and Joe tried to do the same without offending him. His eyes were small and not particularly bright, and he had a mangled ear, like a boxer. The tip of a tattoo peeked up over his collar. Joe also caught sight of scarred and gnarled knuckles before the butler grabbed their bags and headed up the stairs.

The front hall was grand and opened to a double staircase twisting up to a long corridor that ran the length of the entire manor. Sitting rooms jutted off to one side next to them, and on the other was a spectacular dining room. Sheets covered a lot of the furniture and decor, but the entire place was well lit, the opposite to how Joe remembered in the story.

Quick, light footsteps approached and a rotund jolly man spread his arms when he saw the pair. "Ah! You're just in time!"

He stretched his hand out. When Irene ignored it, he turned to Joe, smile never wavering. He shook his hand as if Joe were a film star.

"You must be Doctor Watson. How wonderfully… wonderful! Come, come! The others are here and it's almost time to begin!"

Irene folded her arms. "You said we were to tour the estate and meet your friends."

Dearborn waved his hands. "Yes, we can do all that after!"

"After what?"

"This evening's festivities! You are, after all, the guest of honour, Miss Holmes!"

He spun round and headed off to one of the sitting rooms, leaving the pair to gape after him.

Chapter III

The Problem of the Evening

The voices of at least three or four people, including Dearborn, drifted into the foyer from the sitting room. Irene stayed where she was, however, still in a bit of shock at Dearborn's words. She didn't like festivities on a good day, let alone when they were forced upon her and would surely be something trivial. She had half a mind to snatch her bags and head back to the train station. She had this man's money, and he'd been unclear about his intentions. How could she not have known at the beginning, back at Baker Street that there was more to this? Because Dearborn and his jovial attitude was so overwhelming? Because Joe hadn't been there as a second opinion?

Joe's hand settled on her lower back. Not pushing, but simply supporting whichever way she wanted to move.

A low grunt came from behind them. The butler watched them with his beady eyes, blocking the exit should they choose to make a run for it.

Perhaps whatever was in that room wouldn't be too bad. Perhaps they were all studious people who enjoyed intellectual conversation.

Irene took a deep breath and headed into the room. Five people in total went silent. Two couples, both well into their forties and dressed to the nines, held tall champagne flutes. They looked like any other rich couple, right down to the feather the one woman had in her hair. Neither man looked like a labourer, or that he would've fought under any sort of command during the war. Jobs in finance came to Irene as she took in their pale skin and soft hands.

Dearborn stepped toward her immediately and presented her with a flat palm. "This, ladies and gentlemen, is Miss Irene Holmes. Daughter of Sherlock Holmes."

The quartet murmured, looking at Irene like she was the last jelly roll at the bakery. The lady with the feather stepped forward. When Irene didn't shake her hand, she giggled as if thrilled by her rejection. Dearborn began his introductions then.

"We have Max and Priscilla Prescott, and Doug and Joyce Gillette." When all Irene did was offer them a nod, he chuckled and started into his speech. "Over the course of the next three days, we will be acting out and solving the case of the Hound of the Baskervilles! You will each be assigned a character from the original tale. I've also included my own little twists into the game, but we will be solving a Sherlock Holmes mystery!"

What did he mean they would solve a mystery?

Irene stared, mouth dry, processing the man's words.

"You speak about Sherlock Holmes as if he is a company or a film star," she snapped. "He was not. Also, the mystery of the Baskerville hound was solved. So, are *we* to solve the same case? It is redundant and silly."

The four guests huddled closer as if admiring an animal at the zoo or a circus bear performing a trick. Mr. Dearborn, however, regarded her for a moment before chuckling.

"We are all supporters of Mr. Holmes, and this is a weekend to honour him and all that he has done," he assured. "And with you at the centre of it? Well, it cannot fail!"

Usually, Irene could find any word at any time, but at this moment, she truly couldn't figure out what to say.

True to form, Joe stepped forward, hand on her arm, and addressed Dearborn. "You lured us here under the guise of a case. Not to play a game."

The man hesitated for the briefest of moments, a single eye twitch jumping out. Clearly neither one of them were cooperating with the grand plan, and he seemed like a man that always got what he demanded.

He gave the group a closed-mouth smile and gestured to Joe. "I believe I forgot to introduce Doctor Watson. Joe – not John – this time. Always defending his friend and colleague. Though, this relationship is a bit different than the original duo."

Joe's grip on Irene's arm tightened as the other guests laughed. She needed to take control of whatever was happening here. She had no idea what exactly this "game" entailed, but if they were solve a mystery – especially one that already had a solution – perhaps she should play. If Franklin Dearborn wanted to host a Holmes and a Watson, then that was what he would get.

She folded her arms across her chest and commanded the room.

"We'll play. And then we will leave."

He hesitated again, as if suspicious of her intent, but then he clasped his hands together. "How wonderful! I do believe—"

A loud dinner bell cut him off, but did not deter his enthusiasm.

"Ah, there it is! Dinner! And a glimpse at who everyone will be."

Dearborn ushered them out the far door of the room and toward the dining area. Irene opted to trail behind in order to observe. They passed a large study and the mantle above the fireplace caught her eye. A large painted portrait of her father sat at an angle amongst what looked like pipes, novels and other trinkets. As she stepped into the room to get a better look at the painting, Dearborn called to her.

"Tours will be after dinner, Miss Holmes. Come along."

Joe gently hooked his hand around her arm as they started once again to the dining room.

"You okay?" he whispered.

"I do not like it here."

"Neither do I. We will leave as soon as we've solved whatever game he has for us."

"And not a moment later."

They entered the dining hall and took their place at the heavy wooden table. Real silver adorned the tablecloth and the smell of meat floated in from the kitchen.

Though the guests chittered away to one another, Joe and Irene remained silent. There was something amiss about this whole affair. Besides the obvious trickery to get them here, the butler wasn't the usual hire, and there were no other staff to speak of. There had to be a cook, because someone was preparing some sort of chicken dish. There must also have been a housekeeper or maid, as the place looked rather dust-free.

Every now and then her father's name was mentioned within the conversation, which she did her best to ignore. The guests mostly spoke about the stories, speculating how the crimes could've been different.

In a few moments, a young woman in a maid's uniform exited the kitchen carrying the first course: a cold type of soup. She laid a bowl in front of everyone, but slowed when she got to Irene. Dearborn announced the dinner: a pheasant dish with a *pâté de foie gras* pie, just like it appeared in one of the stories. Irene didn't catch which one, as she studied the maid. Her pupils were dilated a bit too much even for the dim room. As the girl drew her hand away from the soup bowl, Irene caught the dark marks on her wrists. The young maid walked with precise steps, as if moving too fast or carelessly would cause her to topple over. She leaned a little too much on the door as she entered the kitchen, as if needing it for support.

Paper rustling and soup slurping pulled Irene back to the table. Dearborn spoke of an itinerary and a character sheet. Irene forwent the soup, as it was green and looked like pudding. She scooped her own paper; there were a list of activities that she assumed mirrored the original case. Beside her, Joe took a small spoonful of his soup and his jaw tensed as he slowly lowered the utensil back into the bowl, not to be touched again.

While they waited for the pheasant main course, Mr. Dearborn clinked his glass to get everyone's attention. "First, I want to thank you all for being here. It is truly something that we get to act this night out."

The husband of the woman with the feather hat piped up, "Thank you for the invite. Glad we were able to put the incident with the house to bed."

"Quite."

Irene stared at the man, willing him to tell.

He chuckled at her. "We outbid him on the house from the *Greek Interpreter.* You must know that house, eh, Miss Holmes?"

"I do not."

He chuckled again. "Well, anyway, we swooped in at the last minute, didn't we, Frank?"

"You certainly did," Dearborn said through clenched teeth. "Mighty sneakily if you ask me."

"Ah, just a tactic!"

"Just like Max used that tactic of his to steal Priscilla from me!"

"Bought, you mean! My woman likes a three-story house, don't you, sweetheart? Those two-story flats you had just weren't to her taste."

Everyone laughed.

Irene didn't understand. She did know, though, that the half dozen cases they'd solved with the wealthy people in London weren't half as rich as these folk. They bid on houses as if it were some footstool. Their purchases were solely based on whims and beating out other people for fun.

"There are some ground rules," Dearborn continued, "I want this experience to be as fully immersive as possible. Please try to stick to your characters. You may roam around the entire estate, except for the east wing as it is under construction still and therefore dangerous. There should be no need to contact anyone outside of the estate, as we have medic kits and medicine, should something like that happen. Now, let the game begin! To Sherlock Holmes and his studious and incredible daughter. May this weekend bring fun for everyone!"

He lifted his glass and the others followed suit. Irene begrudgingly took her champagne glass and clinked Joe's. The alcohol was sweet but not horrible. Still, she wouldn't sip too much as she wanted to stay alert.

As the maid wheeled a cart of plates out to them, Mr. Dearborn announced the beginning of the game.

"Welcome to you all! Not to frighten anyone, but there have been tales of a mysterious creature lurking, however, those are probably just silly rumours."

The guests started murmuring. Irene caught Joe shoving pheasant into his mouth to keep from laughing.

Dearborn kept speaking, "I hear there's talk of an escaped convict running around these moors!"

"Oh heavens, that is a bit terrifying!" Feather Lady gasped.

"Especially with this hound running around," Doug – or maybe Max – added.

It hadn't even been five minutes of this charade and Irene was already finished with it. "Perhaps the two will meet and the hound will tear the criminal apart then die from over consumption. Then both problems will be gone."

Dearborn laughed. "Your cleverness is unmatched, Holmes! How about we introduce ourselves to one another!"

Irene started into her dinner and was pleasantly surprised by the pheasant. She listened to the introductions and though she hadn't read the story, she heard her father speak on it enough that she knew the people and the outcome. By the time it got around to Joe, she'd solved the mystery.

Her dear friend picked up his paper and sighed. The poor guy clearly wasn't enjoying himself, but he would stick it out as long as Irene did.

He read the card in a rather flat voice. "I am Dr. Watson. I served in the war and am pleased to be visiting with my good friend Holmes."

While others had a big introduction, both hers and Joe's were short, which bothered her more than it should've. They assumed too many things about her father and uncle. Not that she wanted to delve into their personal lives, but these people acted like they knew exactly who Sherlock Holmes and John Watson were.

Her paper simply said:

I am Sherlock Holmes, consulting detective.

"I am…" She trailed off. She wasn't her father, nor would she pretend to be as such. The whole ordeal was a silly re-enactment with no actual crime. Even with Dearborn's added details and attempts at a new mystery, she'd figured it out as soon as everyone started to introduce themselves.

The *only* way Sherlock Holmes would indulge in such a pathetic game would be if there was an actual crime. And right now, the only mystery was the maid and her wrist marks and blank stare. Was there something there? Was it enough to participate?

The money Dearborn paid them was exorbitant, true, but was *that* enough for her to keep going? Even just for one night? After dinner she could always negotiate for more…

Irene found herself wondering what *would* her father do if he were put in this situation? If he was faced with this before she came along, then he would simply walk out. However, after she was born, he'd stay and ensure a higher fee and try to make a case out of the oddly behaved maid.

"Irene?" Joe's soft voice pulled her back to the dining room, and to the eyes watching her with anticipation. She set the card down and cleared her throat. In a posh accent, identical to her father's, she spoke:

"I am Sherlock Holmes, consulting detective and esteemed guest of… whatever his name is. I am sorry to say that there is hardly a case here as everyone has given themselves away with their introductions. It is also obvious, what with this hound and criminal running around, what is going to happen as it is the only possibility.

"This lady with the feather so boldly upon her head will enlist the help of the criminal that wanders the moors to help murder her husband and make it appear as if it were the hound. She would then pay this criminal to swap clothes with her dead spouse and shred his own. He would then walk away with the money.

"How would I know? They were given the first slot of the morning walk and that specific part of the moor to investigate. She also has the persona with the most to gain should her husband die."

As if stuck in time, everyone stared at her unmoving.

Beside her, Joe sighed.

The lady with the feather hat – Joyce? – looked at Dearborn. "Well, is she correct?"

Mr. Dearborn had his gaze fixed on Irene, eyes narrowed in a glare, poorly disguised by a pleasant smile.

Irene stared back. He wanted to play, and play she did. "Of course I am correct."

Dearborn rolled his shoulders as if to reset himself. "You are quite clever, Miss Holmes. But we are still playing out the game because I may have another few tricks up my sleeve! Now, please, everyone finish up and we shall retire to the study for a brief time before we tuck into bed!"

* * * * *

The rest of dinner went on quietly – at least for Joe and Irene. Soon everyone sat around the study. The pair remained standing, however.

Irene stood in front of the fireplace loaded with Sherlock Holmes paraphernalia: a pen he supposedly wrote with; a replica of a pipe to which she remembered him throwing out when she was quite little; a stone from Reichenbach falls – the place he faked his own death. All precious things to a collector, but to her, they were cheap nods to stories he'd left behind.

And the portrait was a caricature, surely. The long face and hooked nose of her father was present, but his eyes were too sunken and he had a frown on his face, which he only ever had when he was tired or disappointed.

Perhaps she should be grateful to people like Dearborn for keeping her father's memory alive. If he wasn't such a smug individual, she might have been. But he wanted to treat her uncle's writing like fiction. Did they not realise this was a living person who'd gone through some of those troubling stories? That the person they worshipped was living out the rest of his life with no memory of half the life he'd led?

None of this felt like an homage to her father. It was the whim of a man with too much money wanting to live a different lifestyle.

Her tenseness must've shown, because Joe's hand came to rest on her arm. Meanwhile, Dearborn was talking and holding a copy of Holmes' stories.

"This, my friends, is a copy signed by Dr. John Watson himself."

This caught Irene's attention. She didn't remember her uncle ever signing his work. Her father would have certainly rolled his eyes.

"May I see?" she asked.

Dearborn grinned at her, delighted she was participating. He handed her the book and she studied the signature.

"This is not signed by Dr. Watson." She handed it back. "He never lifted his pen from the letters. It is a very good replica, but it is not his."

A vein in Dearborn's neck twitched and he set the book back on the shelf. He motioned to the two empty chairs that Joe and Irene had yet to occupy. "Why don't you both sit and tell us some stories about Sherlock and Dr. Watson. You must have some incredible anecdotes about them!"

The other guests came to attention and spoke all at once:

"Is it true you are living back at 221b? Right on Baker Street?"

"When was the last time you spoke to Sherlock?"

"Oh, she probably speaks to him all the time!"

"Sherlock doesn't still live there, does he?"

"Oh, to see Sherlock Holmes and Dr Watson at Baker Street!"

A tightness started in Irene's chest, akin to how Joe described his episodes. Her breathing quickened. She tried to calmly reach out for her friend but couldn't find him. They continued to lob questions at her. She could hear Joe in the distance fielding them and deflecting. Her heart thudded so hard, she feared it might explode, so she let her anger react instead.

"If you people want to know more about him, then read Dr. Watson's stories." She balled her fists and dared them to interrupt her. "If you think you know him so well, you'd know he wouldn't stand for this farce. He would call you all insufferable idiots to your faces, then would retire to his room. Which is exactly what I am going to do."

She pivoted on her heel and started for the stairs. The pompous lunatics called after her, but Joe intervened, repeating her sentiments about retiring for the night. No one but her friend came after her as she ascended the stairs. He caught up to her quickly and took her arm in his.

"Hey, slow down."

They stopped at the top. She didn't realise how fast she was breathing until Joe put his hands on her shoulders.

"Irene, look at me."

She stared into his blue eyes, tracing the dark ring around the bright iris. She tried to focus on his words, but they were jumbled. He was breathing deeply, though. Purposefully. She started breathing with him. In and out. In. Out. She cleared her throat, cheeks warming at how out of control her body was.

"I am fine now," she said, voice softer than she wanted. "Let's just go to our room. Though, I do not know which one it is."

"I asked Dearborn before I came after you." Joe held out his arm and she grasped it. He led her to the last room at the end of the hallway, on the side of the house that faced the moors.

By the time they reached the room, she'd shaken off the panicked feeling and was ready to sleep away this horrid day and leave on the first train. Their accommodation was spacious enough, with a large bed in the middle of two small windows. An en-suite lavatory was attached to the room, to which Irene headed to immediately to splash some cold water on her face. As she passed the window, however, she paused.

Bars were secured to the frame, with no way of opening them.

"Oh." Joe drew her attention. "There is only one bed."

"It's the bars on the window that should worry you more," she said, then glanced behind her. "That bed is more than big enough for both of us."

"Irene, we can't share a bed."

"Why? We fall asleep in the living room together all the time."

He ran a hand through his hair. "This is a bed. It's... more intimate."

Tired, frustrated and simply over the day, she gestured to the room. "Who is here to say anything? No one. Also, what do you think is going to happen? Our pyjamas will disappear and we will suddenly form a pretzel with each other's limbs? I have no plans for that. I am going to sleep, then leaving this place as soon as daylight hits."

As she shut the lavatory door behind her, she slumped her shoulders. She should've been nicer to Joe. His qualms with only having one bed were understandable. Irene recognised it as inappropriate to share a bed with someone one was not in a relationship with, let alone someone who was in a long-term commitment with someone else. But how would she solve the situation? Neither of them would sleep on the floor, as that would be uncomfortable. The state of this place, though tidy, was old and lacked a thorough clean.

Once she'd refreshed herself, Irene found Joe in blue striped pyjamas turning down the covers on the bed.

"I am sorry for my earlier words," she said, digging out her own, similarly striped navy pyjamas. "I understand why this is inappropriate."

He shook his head and fluffed one of the two pillows as he turned away to let her change. "It's not your fault. It's my own insecurities."

"I thought Sarah loved you."

"She does… That's the problem."

Perhaps because she'd been made a fool all night, or because she was tired – or maybe because she needed to get some feelings off her chest – Irene decided to speak her mind. Well, more of her mind than she usually did.

She stuffed her clothes into her bag. "I am finished changing. Also, may I make an observation?"

Joe looked like he hadn't slept in ages. "Sure."

"You are never happy when you are with Sarah, I mean not truly. You often lie to her about your whereabouts or omit things altogether. If you are to marry her, then I think that you would end up miserable. But perhaps I am wrong and simply being mean. I do like Sarah. She is almost what I would call a friend, and I wouldn't want any ill-will to come to her. But I like you more and you are just simply not happy. Again, perhaps I have no idea how relationships work and perhaps you are elated when you are with her. But that is just what I see of my best friend. Now, I have felt enough feelings today to last me a month, and have told off everyone including you. So, I am going to sleep now. Goodnight, Joe."

She climbed into the bed and pulled the fresh covers up to her chin, curling beneath them. Joe sighed, long and tired and full of some worry she probably gave to him.

"Goodnight, Irene.

Chapter IV
A True Mystery in Baskerville Hall

Joe stared at the ceiling. He'd been drifting in and out for the past few hours, listening to Irene sleep soundly beside him. Tonight had been a whirlwind and he was worried his friend was going to simply explode. Tomorrow morning, the first order of business was to get some breakfast and get on a train home.

A light flashed outside the window.

He didn't think much of it, until it flashed again.

Joe climbed out of bed, catching the time on the clock on the wall: almost three. Wonderful.

Two torches flashed near the forest's entrance at the back of the estate.

From the bed, Irene grunted, "What is happening?"

"Lights upon the moor. Like the original story. In the morning, we will all discuss what it could possibly mean…"

He trailed off as he looked at her. She'd taken most of the covers, her hair was an absolute mess and her eyes were barely open. There was a large dent next to her where he had laid. The whole image heated his cheeks and made his stomach twitter. He looked back outside as Irene sighed and crawled out of the bed.

"What an act," she scoffed and went back under the covers. "They aren't even doing anything with the torches. They are just waving them about. They could've at least made it seem like people were looking for something. Tomorrow we will try to speak with the maid, if those marks haven't faded and her eyes are glassy again. Otherwise, I am ready to go home. Goodnight again, Joe."

He took one last look at the torches and rubbed his eyes. "Goodnight again, Irene."

* * * * *

Joe woke as the early morning sun shone through the barred window. His feet were intertwined with Irene's and their backs rested against each other. His friend still slept peacefully. He very carefully extracted himself from her clutches and slid out of bed. Her words from last night echoed in his head. She was so astute at mysteries and small clues and details, but feelings – especially those of others – were not her strength. So, for her to notice how sullen he'd become meant he needed to deal with the situation.

Her reflection on his relationship with Sarah was not wholly incorrect. It was a truth he'd been avoiding. He'd said to himself many times that he needed to seriously think about them and once he was home, he would. Even if that meant the end.

Or surging forward.

His mother's ring sat on his bedside table, waiting for him to decide. Perhaps Baker Street was the limbo he needed to get out of.

That thought churned his stomach as he grabbed his shaving cream from his bag. He removed his pyjama shirt and started painting his face, trying to keep his mind on their current situation. As he drew the last stroke of white cream, he heard Irene knock on the door.

"Joe? If you are only shaving at the moment, may I take my hairbrush? I fear these curls will never be tamed unless I start now."

He opened the door to let her in. Irene startled at his appearance. She looked him up and down, lips pursed as if hiding a smile or laughter. His cheeks heated. He looked down to make sure he still had trousers on, or if there was anything to cause her to giggle.

"What is it? What is wrong?"

"Oh nothing," she said, eyes still crinkling as she held back a giggle. "Your body structure is quite lovely, especially for a bookworm. But I have never seen skin this pale in my life. Even mine has some colour to it."

Joe put his hand across his chest as if to hide his skin. "It is wintertime in England! Of course I am pale."

She squeezed behind him and poked his shoulder. "You are beyond pale. The shaving cream is the same colour as you. You are a beacon to be put on a hill to guide people to the town."

Joe snorted at her, little white dots of shaving cream flying onto the mirror. "Shall I critique you? Your massive head of hair? The crease line on your face from the pillow? I'm sure if you showed me your body, you'd be just as pale—" He cut his words at her raised brow. "I did not mean to ask you to remove your clothes. I am going back to shaving."

She grinned at him – a rare thing for her to do nowadays, her smile stretching and crinkling her eyes and lighting up her still-tired face. She left him to his task.

Joe rolled his eyes at the absurdity of it all.

It didn't take either of them long to finish getting ready for the day, or to pack their cases for a quick exit.

"I am not sure what to do if the maid is in the state she was yesterday," Irene said.

"We either stay and investigate her, or leave regardless of what her condition is."

They started down the hall to the stairs when something caught Irene's eye on the other couple's room. A lock on the outside of their door. It was unlocked, but interesting, nonetheless.

Joe looked at the other couple's door.

It was the same.

"Curious," Irene said. "Our door does not have a lock."

"Maybe it's leftover? Perhaps it means nothing."

"Perhaps it means everything."

"In regard to what?"

She shrugged. "I don't know, but I can smell bacon and I am hungry. Let's eat, then leave."

Mr. Dearborn and one of the couples – Joe couldn't remember their names, only that they owned horses and bred collies – were already sat at the table in the dining area. The couple who wore the feathers were noticeably absent and he tried to figure out if that was part of the original story or if they were still in bed.

The maid came out with a tray of dishes filled to the brim with bacon, eggs, breads, and fruits. She had the same bruises on her wrists, and her eyes were still glazed over, as if she were high on some drug. She placed a plate in front of Joe and he tucked in immediately. Irene looked ready to investigate or start a conversation with the maid, and he wanted to be ready for whatever that brought to the day. So, a full stomach was needed.

"Thank you," Irene said, and Joe realised she was the only one to thank the maid during both meals. "What is your name?"

The maid looked like a rabbit being discovered. She glanced at Dearborn then mumbled, "Mary."

"Did you work for Mr. Dearborn previously or are you new to his staff?"

"I, um…"

"Mary," Dearborn interjected. "We could use some more orange juice."

Irene touched the girl's arm but addressed Dearborn. "We were having a conversation. Please answer me, Mary."

But the girl stayed silent. She looked at her employer again as tears welled in her eyes. He flicked his hand and she scampered off.

"So sorry," Dearborn said, back to his jovial self. "She is still new."

The rich woman across from them woman rolled her eyes. "Oh, I know what you mean. We had one that would constantly giggle. Remember her, Max?"

Her husband shrugged. "We go through so many of them."

While they chatted about not finding good help these days, Irene leaned into Joe. "We are staying. At least until we figure out what is going on."

Joe shoved another piece of bacon in his mouth, nodding.

When everyone was about halfway through their meal, the butler wandered in and Dearborn gestured to him.

"Ah, Morris! You look like you have news for us."

He nodded and uttered a line that was clearly rehearsed: "The Gillettes are not in their room. And they are not anywhere in the building."

Dearborn gasped and looked at the others at the table. "Oh no! I wonder if they are missing!"

The wife – Priscilla, Joe was sure – gasped. "You know what? I did see torches outside last night, as if someone were out there!"

Her husband nodded beside her. "Perhaps a walk around the moors after breakfast is needed! See what we can find!"

Joe looked at Irene to see if this new development changed the plan for staying here. She shovelled food into her mouth and looked utterly annoyed as she spoke between bites:

"This would be the wife who is supposed to murder her husband, correct?"

"What an idea, Holmes," Dearborn exclaimed. "We will just have to find out!"

"We have not interviewed your staff yet. That is an important step in any case. It is imperative to acquire more information. Perhaps about a hound and a criminal on the run."

Dearborn shook his head. "No need for that right now. We must get out to the moors."

"It is important to the case," Irene argued. "I must speak to them at some point."

"You may certainly do so, just not right now."

Joe thought she might argue again, but she finished her eggs and stood. "To the moors, then."

Pivoting, Irene headed out of the dining area. Joe took the last chug of his orange juice and followed her from the room. She waited in the foyer as Morris gathered their jackets and boots. The rest of them joined and they all tugged on their outdoor gear.

The morning air was cold and biting. Despite being ready first, Joe and Irene trailed behind Dearborn and the Prescotts.

"Do you truly think he convinced that couple to wake early and be out here for us to find?" Joe asked.

Irene snorted. "They probably volunteered before he ever had to ask. What happened in the original story?"

"There are stone huts on the property that someone was living in. Turns out it was the—"

"Escaped convict?"

Joe nodded.

"Ah, so I am expecting to see some…" She trailed off as the stone huts came into view.

Priscilla Prescott squealed, "Just like in the story!"

"Of course it is," Irene said. "The story is fact."

The couple rushed ahead to the hut and the woman declared after a second, "There are clothes in here!"

Mr. Prescott exclaimed just as excitedly, "It's clear someone is living here! And these look just like a prison uniform."

Priscilla gasped. "But why would a convict stay here? And the hound! We haven't discussed the hound!"

Irene scoffed. "There is absolutely no evidence of a hound. Not a footprint, tuft of fur, nothing. I deem there is no hound."

"There is a hound," Dearborn said. "The reports have been quite numerous. Perhaps you should keep looking in the other huts! Or around them!"

Mumbling under her breath, Irene headed the opposite way, toward the tree line of the forest and crouched down. Joe opted to stick by her, wandering behind, waiting for a command like he would on a normal case. This time, however, he tried to enjoy the grounds and the ominous building at the top of the hill. Though the morning was cold, the day was warming up, bringing a touch of fog. It was high right now, but in an hour, it would settle on the grass and make the whole scene one from a horror novel.

"Curious," Irene muttered, keeping her voice low. "The Gillettes' footprints. Both of them off into the woods. Stumbling around."

"As if drunk?" Joe whispered back, still feigning looking around. Given Irene's volume level, she wanted to keep this discovery quiet for now.

"Perhaps," she said, waddling forward and poking the grass. "Or drugged."

"Or forced to walk?"

"If forced by a weapon or a brute, they'd be straighter."

She stood and looked at him through furrowed brows and determination she usually had when working a case. This was the first time he'd seen this expression on her all weekend.

"What if the torches we saw last night weren't being waved as a ploy and instead were held by a drunk or drugged person? That pattern, or non-pattern rather, matches exactly what we saw."

"So, what happened? They got drunk, wandered outside and that happens to fit the narrative of the story? They were drugged and pushed outside? This game just took a drastic turn if either of those are true."

Dearborn called to them as the others moved away from the huts. "Holmes! Watson! What are you two discussing? Please do share!"

Neither one of them had time to come up with an answer, though. Priscilla shrieked, the sound shrill and loud, breaking through the morning fog. She pointed at something behind Joe and Irene as her face paled.

Chapter V
A Body in the Moors

Irene spun around to the cause of the woman's shriek. While she wasn't expecting a hound, what she saw did give her pause.

Mrs. Gillette stumbled out from the forest, wheezing and coughing. Her night gown was torn and filthy, her shoes missing. Small scratches from tree branches and bramble adorned her bare arms. She dry-heaved as if all the sick were already expelled. Both Irene and Joe rushed forward to help her. As they approached, she collapsed to the ground.

"It got him," she wailed. "The hound got him! It's here! It's real!"

Joe recoiled. Irene stayed steady, however, though her stomach flipped at the sight. The woman's pupils were the size of saucers, almost covering the blue in her eyes. Her eyelids twitched and her tongue bled from her mouth as if she'd clamped down on it without knowing. She smelled like dirt and blood and vomit.

"Where is your husband," Irene asked her. "Where is…"

"Doug," Joe hissed.

"Where is Doug?"

The woman pointed into the woods.

By this point, the other couple, Dearborn, and the butler had arrived. Morris scooped up Mrs. Gillette and started to the house.

"No," Irene yelled after them. "Bring her. I may need her help."

Dearborn intervened. "Holmes, she is clearly not well, she—"

"Must stay with us," Irene snapped. There was no way she was letting that woman out of her sight. She had no idea what kind of drugs she was on, but Dearborn had to be the supplier and she didn't trust Mrs Gillette to be left alone.

Irene started into the woods with Joe behind her. Thankfully, Morris stayed at the edge of the trees, holding Mrs. Gillette tight.

The other couple followed the pair, murmuring excitedly. With every step, Irene's anger grew. Had Dearborn really drugged and injured a guest for the sake of a game?

She found the broken branches and footprints easily enough and as they approached a small ravine, Mrs. Gillette shrieked again.

"Careful of the hound! This is where we were!"

"You." Irene pointed to Mr. Prescott. "Go with the butler back to the house and ring an ambulance."

Even though she'd demanded it, the man didn't move. "I would like to see what is down that cliff."

"A woman is injured!" Irene snapped.

"I see something down there! A body!" his wife called, leaning over the rocks.

Irene rushed to her and peered down as well. Mr. Gillette lay face down in the leaves and twigs. She looked along the rocks, searching for an easy way down.

Dearborn shouted above the commotion. "This has taken a turn! We must all get inside before the hound comes back!"

"There is no hound," Irene cried.

"Miss Holmes. We must move on with the story. Morris will collect him once we are inside discussing the clues."

She ignored him and started down the rocks. The man yelled something at Joe and she heard her friend respond with a curt "no" as he came to the top of the rocks to watch her. She heard commotion from above as Dearborn tried to usher the others away from the ravine and to the house. Irene didn't stop to see if she was being observed as she approached the body. She checked his pulse and wasn't surprised when she felt none.

Mr. Gillette was most certainly dead, had been for hours now. She looked up at Joe and shook her head.

"Ring for the ambulance," he shouted at the people above. "What are you doing? Now!"

Irene left him to deal with Dearborn as she observed the body. Mr. Gillette's eyes were popped open and bloodshot, and his skin was pale and wet from the ground. His nose had bled before he died and there was still vomit around his mouth. If he wasn't laying at the bottom of a cliff, his death would be consistent with an overdose of drugs.

What was even more curious, though, was the ground around him. There were no struggle marks, telling her that he fell from the cliff. However, there were no injuries consistent with a fall. If he fell over the edge while still alive, even if he was drugged, there would be signs he tensed before hitting the ground. But his coat was askew and his back was dotted with leaves and twigs.

As if someone rolled him off the rocks.

"Joe," she called.

He helped her up and hissed in her ear, "This is not good. Everyone is agitated."

"They should be. Has an ambulance been called?"

"No one would leave, and I didn't want to leave you down there alone."

The Prescotts rushed her, bombarding her with questions, but Dearborn stepped in.

"Let's all leave the woods, hm?"

Morris stood at the top of the hill beside Mrs Gillette who rocked against the house.

Mr. Prescott looked at Irene. "Do we really need an ambulance?"

"We need both an ambulance and a coroner. That man is dead and has been since last night."

Prescott turned to Dearborn. "Is this true? Tell me this isn't part of the game, Frank?"

"It is all part of it! Do not fret!"

"A dead man," Irene snapped. "How is that part of it?"

He stepped toward her, but Joe blocked him. Still, he yelled, "You shouldn't have gone down that hill. That wasn't part of the plan."

"Was the plan murder?"

He stepped forward again but Joe shoved him away. "Back off. Whatever this is, it's over."

Irene turned to Mr. Prescott. "Go ring an ambulance."

Priscilla stepped forward. "I will go to Joyce."

The couple ran off as Joe and Irene prepared to confront Dearborn again.

He, however, waved at Morris, then gestured to Mr. Prescott. "Stop him."

Determined to leave this place as fast as possible, Irene hooked her arm in Joe's and they started toward the estate.

A gun shot cracked the air and echoed through the moors.

Irene and Joe both dropped to the ground. He covered her head with his arms, but a second shot never came.

Dearborn groaned. "You weren't supposed to *shoot* him, just stop him."

The pair straightened. Mr Prescott bled out on the grass a mere two metres from the side steps of the estate. Priscilla shrieked and rushed forward to her husband, flinging herself on his body.

Irene tried to step in front of Joe to address Dearborn, but her friend had the same idea. They both tripped over each other's feet and Joe caught her before she fell.

Dearborn sighed, his jovial persona gone completely.

Morris had his pistol now aimed at the pair, as the host gestured to the house. "Both of you, inside. Now."

Chapter VI

The East Wing of Baskerville Hall

Joe's heart thrummed in his ears, which were still ringing from the gun shot. He needed to either get the revolver's aim away from Irene, or get her away from the gun. She looked ready to fight both Dearborn and his butler, and Joe had a feeling she might win.

Priscilla sobbed over her husband, wailing and screaming profanities at Morris. The butler passed the gun to Dearborn.

He gestured to the house again. "Inside, both of you."

Morris scooped up Priscilla. She pounded her fists into his back, but he carried her like a ragdoll into the manor.

Mrs. Gillette had completely shut down. She slumped against the house, eyelids drooping.

Dearborn motioned yet again with the pistol. "We shall meet in the study to discuss the clues."

Joe put his hand on Irene's back, urging her forward. If he could get her inside and potentially alone – or at least away from Morris –they could figure out their next steps.

"To the study," Dearborn commanded.

Irene dragged her feet, but after an encouraging push from Joe, she started on her way. He hated how he was forcing her to comply, but it was their best chance for making it out of this situation. Dearborn was clearly not above killing people. Would he kill the daughter of Sherlock Holmes? Probably not. But Joe felt like he was fair game at this point. The only thing he shared with the original Holmes and Watson was a common last name and his proximity to Irene.

They reached the study.

Dearborn stopped them in the middle of the room. "Here is where we discuss the evidence—"

"There was no evidence," Irene bit out. "Not of a hound, nor a criminal. You simply drugged *and* murdered them!"

Dearborn sighed again, hair frazzled. He waved the pistol around with the ease of a child with a plaything. "Someone *had* to die, right? That's what's needed for the story. That's what's needed for Holmes to solve the case!"

"Sherlock Holmes isn't here," Irene shouted at him.

Joe winced.

"Clearly, he isn't," Dearborn snarled, but the gun remained at his side, thankfully.

He took a moment to compose himself, brushing his hair to the side and fixing his vest. The door behind him opened and Morris walked in.

"I'm having trouble."

"So?"

"I need more hands."

Dearborn looked at Joe and Irene as if he was going to let one of them go. Joe grabbed his best friend's wrist. He wasn't leaving her, regardless of what their so-called host said. When he pointed the gun at them again, Joe gripped Irene tighter, attempting to tug her behind him.

"Both of you will stay here and discuss the case. I will be back momentarily. Do not try to get out, please. The window will not open and this door will be locked. I hate to do it, but we must finish this mystery."

He strode from the room, slamming the door. The click of a lock filled the silence.

Joe ran a hand through his hair, sweating in his coat.

Irene, however, didn't move. She stared at the mantle full of Sherlock Holmes items, jaw clenched, cheeks red with anger.

Joe undid his coat, letting some cool air in.

"Irene. Either undo your jacket, or take it off. You'll get overheated."

She either didn't hear him or chose to ignore him, eyes fixed to the portrait of her father. "We need to see what he's keeping in that east wing."

"East wing?" Joe looked at her, bewildered. "Forget about the east wing. We need to leave or find a way to ring Lestrade."

"What if he's keeping those women in there? What if…" She trailed off and glanced at the portrait again.

"We can retrieve whatever items you want later."

"And what of the women?"

"Since when are you so keen on saving people?"

Her eyes widened. Joe sighed.

"I am sorry, Irene. But we need to escape."

"We are surrounded by fields. If we run, they may shoot us out in the open."

"Then we ring Lestrade."

"You go ring him and I'll—"

"I am not leaving you."

"Then the east wing it is."

She shook her coat off and pulled a pin from her hair as she strode toward the door. She worked the lock until it clicked open.

Silence greeted them once the door opened and Irene rushed across the hall to the stairs.

Cussing under his breath, Joe followed.

The hallway to the rooms in the east wing was dark and full of cobwebs. The bedrooms on this side were all open and empty, except for the room at the very end of the hall. The door was locked when Irene tried it, to which Joe was relieved. They needed to get out of the building and—

Irene pulled two more pins from her hair and started on the lock.

"Dammit, Irene. We shouldn't be here. We have to go."

"I must see what's in here."

She got the door to open easily and silently. In the middle of the room was a large table with a lamp on it. Bookshelves adorned the far wall, stuffed with hats, coats, pipes and replicas of various Sherlock Holmes items. The bottom shelf was lined with busts of Napoleon, and one shelf had a collection of red wigs. There wasn't a speck of dust on anything, as if each item was thoroughly cared for or used often.

Irene stood at the large table, head down, entranced by whatever she'd found. Joe peered over her shoulder and his hand went to his mouth.

A map of their neighbourhood was stuck in the middle, with a pin on 221 Baker Street. A dozen photographs of them over the past two years were spread out. They were having dinner at the pub. Exiting The Ritz after visiting with the American film stars. Irene walking Isla down Baker Street. Joe leaving a bookshop.

"What is this?" he asked, rocks sitting in his stomach.

"He has been keeping track of us like he kept track of my father."

Surrounding the photographs were Sherlock Holmes articles from the past forty years. Cases he'd solved, when he'd been spotted out in London, about his death, then sudden reappearance.

Irene touched a collection of articles with headlines like:

Famous Detective Seen with Daughter!

Sherlock Holmes Married?

There were articles speculating on where he went after Dr. Watson stopped writing the stories, and if he was even still alive.

Irene picked up a piece of paper and Joe heard her take a ragged breath. In her shaking hands was her uncle's obituary.

Joe needed to get her out of here as fast as possible, even if he had to carry her. He laid an arm gently around her shoulder and wrapped his other hand around hers to keep her fingers from shaking.

"Let's go. Grab our bags and run. We can ring Lestrade from a pub in town."

He tugged her but she resisted. She wasn't listening to him, which would not bode well.

A door slammed from down the stairs and heavy footsteps marched around frantically.

"Irene, let's go," Joe pleaded, but she wouldn't budge. He released her and shut the door to the room, closing off the light source from the hall.

"No!" Irene cried. "I can't see him."

Dearborn shouted from the stairs and Joe grabbed for Irene. She wiggled away, though, and started gathering papers from the desk.

"Irene, we must go."

"I want to burn it all."

He wasn't sure if she was speaking to him or herself, but it didn't matter. Joe ran to the window and flung back the heavy curtains, shining light into the room again. There were no bars covering the glass and he easily flicked the latch. The windowpane swung open, but looking at the drop below made his stomach lurch. There was a small ledge that led to piping down the house. If they could just shimmy over them and down, they'd be home free.

He just had to get Irene away from that table.

The door burst open and Morris stormed into the room, aiming right for her. Joe launched himself away from the window and made it between them in only a few strides.

He shouldered the large man's stomach, but it didn't do much. He pushed Joe aside as if he weighed nothing, but Joe hooked their arms together. Stumbling, Morris tripped over Joe's feet and they both collapsed to the ground. The butler swung but Joe dodged, and the man's hand went into the wood floor. Joe tried to get a foot between them to kick Morris off, but his body was too big. The butler swung again. Joe turned his head but it was too late. The fist connected with the side of his head, producing instant stars. Joe rolled over, dizzy, attempting to stand. Large hands grabbed his shoulders, dragging him to his feet. Then a hand went around his neck. He gagged, struggling to breath, clawing at the butler's arm. The man shuffled backwards, taking Joe from the room.

He tried to call out for Irene, but his voice was hoarse.

As darkness closed in around him, he saw Dearborn move toward his friend.

Chapter VII

Continuing with the Mystery

Irene knew Joe wanted her to leave. She knew she *should* leave. But she couldn't. Her whole life, her father's and uncle's, were laid out in front of her. Or at least it was until Joe shut the door. But, then, he must've opened it again because she could see everything lit up once more.

She wanted to destroy it.

But she also wanted to gather it all up and take it back home.

A scuffle sounded behind her, but she couldn't drag her eyes from all the papers.

Then, pudgy fingers that definitely weren't Joe's wrapped around her arm. She dropped the photographs and swung, connecting with Franklin Dearborn's nose. He stumbled back, hand over his face as blood seeped through his fingers.

Beyond him, Joe lay in the hallway, eyes closed, unmoving. A thousand cuss words flew through her head as she rushed forward to her friend. A large arm snatched her mid-stride and another went around her throat. The butler's moth-ball smell reached her nose.

She elbowed him in the stomach and kicked his instep, but he held tight. She coughed, gagging, and scratched his arm, skin curling under her fingernails.

She wouldn't last.

But she had to.

She reached up and tried to find his eyes, but all she caught was his cheek. She swiped at it anyway, drawing more blood.

Spots appeared in her vision and her arms grew weak. Still, she kicked and tried to scream until it was too late, and she slipped into darkness.

* * * * *

Her head ached. Her mouth was dry as if stuffed with cotton. After a few blinks, her vision cleared.

She was slumped forward and tied to a chair, her arms behind her. Her left bicep hurt as if she'd been jagged with a needle.

She was awake but still groggy. No doubt she'd been drugged. But a small dose, probably just enough to keep her sedated while they got her to the study and tied her up.

She faced the mantle full of Sherlock Holmes items and the portrait with its dead eyes and too big nose.

She blinked some more and shook her head.

Joe sat on the floor next to the fireplace, hands and feet bound, head resting against the brick. He blinked slowly, eyes glazed, obviously infused with twice the amount of sedative they'd given her.

Dearborn paced in front of the fire, hands clasped behind his back. It looked unnatural, as if he'd adopted this pose after mimicking someone. His nose had stopped bleeding, but the bruising had already started. He looked at her, and upon realising she was awake, grinned.

"Ah, welcome back, Miss Holmes. You have been naughty! Just like the original Holmes! Are you ready to continue the story?"

"There is no story." Irene's voice was hoarse and she cleared her throat. "You are a madman."

"I am only mad for Sherlock Holmes. And his wonderful stories."

She strained against the binds but they didn't budge. "If you are so infatuated with him, then why tie up his daughter? What is your purpose?"

"My purpose? My only purpose is to preserve the Holmes tales and ensure his legacy is passed down! Doctor Watson was such a good writer. He put us right there in the action and the mystery. I could only *dream* of writing stories as good. Tell me, does he have any unfinished tales? Any that were never published? If so, I would gladly make sure they see the light of day!"

"I don't know," she said, half-truthfully. Her father solved hundreds of cases, so her uncle probably had notes of most of them tucked away somewhere. His belongings, however, had stayed with her father out on the farm. She had no desire to sort through them.

Dearborn shook his head, disappointed, then continued to pace.

Joe wiggled on the floor, drugged, and sore. He finally focused on her and his eyes widened. He opened his mouth, then worked his jaw as if it were sore.

Dearborn didn't see him, or didn't care, as he addressed her again. He had a mad look in his eye that made Irene lean back into the chair.

"You know," he began, "I took the liberty of writing my own story."

She didn't know whether to laugh or scream. Her father wasn't some fictional character to be tossed into any old story. And her uncle's writing was solely unique. It would take an author of exceptional talent to recreate the cases her father solved.

Could it be done? Most likely.

But certainly not by this man.

He dug through some papers on his desk and sauntered over to her. "It is not finished yet, but I believe it is one of the better Holmes stories."

He held the first page out to her.

Irene refused to read a single word. She gleaned her father's name a few times and felt bile rise in her throat. The man shook the papers at her, and that bile turned to hot fire. She spat on the papers, leaving a large glob of saliva. The ink ran down the sheets, the words meshing into each other. Dearborn backhanded her. The large ring on his finger connected with her cheekbone drawing blood.

Irene bit her tongue, refusing to cry out at the pain. From behind Dearborn, Joe yelled something incoherent and struggled to his feet. Morris strode over to him and threw him back to the ground. He wiggled against his own bindings, chest heaving and eyes wide.

Irene recognised it. The start of one of his panic-induced episodes leftover from the war where he had been taken prisoner. They'd done unspeakable things to him, some of which he hadn't even told Irene because he claimed they were simply lost from his mind. Joe looked at her then, trying to find some comfort, but he was across the room, bound and drugged.

She needed to put a stop to whatever Dearborn was doing. And that meant either overtaking him or playing into his game. Her stomach churned at the thought of cooperating with him yet again.

Joe coughed and writhed against the fireplace. She could withstand whatever Dearborn threw at her, but she couldn't bear to see her friend like this. Tears pricked her eyes as she watched him heave another breath.

She needed to get him loose and out of here.

"Let him go. You want to continue this story, then you need a Holmes *and* a Watson."

Dearborn waved him aside. "I don't need *that* Watson."

"The other one is dead. So unless you search the city registry for another, that's the only one you have. I will not continue without him."

"You don't *need* him, though, not truly. The more I think about it, I wonder if the original Holmes needed his Watson?"

He didn't believe his own words, Irene could see it in his eyebrow twitch and gaze shooting to Joe.

"If you think any differently, then you didn't understand the stories, or their relationship at all. Release Joe and do not take him from my side or I shall become unbearable."

As he considered her, the urge to strangle the man had never been stronger.

"Very well, Holmes," he finally said, then turned to Morris. "I have to go get the next part of the game ready. Untie her, but keep him like this."

Morris went to Joe. He tried to move away, pressing his body against the fireplace, but the butler dragged him to his feet.

Before leaving the room, Dearborn paused to address Irene. "I don't want to have to alter your mind because I need it sharp. But him? I can keep him like this for a long time."

He strode from the room with all the confidence of a man that won.

Morris cut the ropes around Joe's ankles and wrists, and shoved him toward the door. Joe stumbled, nearly falling on Irene. He clutched the chair to keep himself upright. The butler tugged at him but he held fast to the chair and shook his head.

"No."

The butler grunted in frustration, then punched Joe in the stomach. He cried out, keeling over, but his hand remained clamped to the chair.

"Release me," Irene said. "And we will both go easily with you."

The butler did as told and cut the ties holding Irene to the chair. Once freed, she grabbed Joe's arm and he released the chair. She wrapped a hand around his waist, causing him to wince.

Morris went ahead and opened the door. Joe pressed his face to hers, his mouth at her ear.

"Tattoo," he hissed, words slurred. "Marine. Tattoo. Neck. American."

He sighed, as if that took all his energy, but he did look pointedly at the butler. Irene had thought she heard an accent, but she had yet to figure out if it was just Morris talking low and slow, or if he really wasn't from England. She trusted Joe's knowledge of military tattoos, even in his current state. He'd met all kinds of soldiers during the war, and no doubt grew to memorise the good ones.

However, no matter who this man served, he was not good anymore. Although, he didn't seem too thrilled to be doing this job... It was as if he hurt people and followed Dearborn's command because he owed the wealthy man a debt or two.

Joe leaned on her all the way to the dining room. Dearborn sat at his spot at the head of the table, jovial smile upon his round, sweaty face. Irene got her partner to his seat, then took her own place beside him.

Their host waved the butler over and whispered something in his ear, before the man hurried away.

Joe's hands rested on his lap, palm upturned, as he gazed at her. She had no idea what he wanted, but reached out for his hand under the table and intertwined her fingers in his. It seemed to soothe him. He blinked and shook his head.

The maid came out and though still slightly glazed, her eyes widened in horror when she saw them. They had to look an awful sight. Joe with his cut lip, bobbing head, bruised eye and stoned pupils looked horrific to Irene, and she had seen him beat up before. Her face fared better, but the cut from Dearborn's ring felt sticky and dry all at once.

The maid set the plates in front of them and quickly left.

"I shall speak as we eat," Dearborn informed them. "We need to reel this case in and tie up all the loose ends!"

Irene's mind moved a hundred kilometres a second as she tried to figure a way out of this. She could outrun Dearborn and probably Morris, but Joe wouldn't keep up – not in his condition. She couldn't fight them. To win that, she'd need a weapon.

And she really didn't want to play out the rest of the case. She didn't even know how the original story went. She tried to remember her father telling her about it. Was there another body? Did they go back outside to the moors at all? If so, she might be able to get away with Joe.

She heard the maid cough from the kitchen and thought of a risky but life-saving plan.

"It would help if I had a notebook," she said to Dearborn. "You've rendered my note-taker immobile and unable to assist me. So, I will have to do it myself."

He hesitated, fiddling with his fork, but finally waved at Morris. "Get her a book."

The butler disappeared and came back moments later with a small notepad and a pen. As he handed it to her, Dearborn commanded him to go check on the other women.

Irene wrote the telephone number for DI Lestrade with his name, then scribbled beneath it, furrowing her brown. "This pen is not working. May I have another? Or a pencil, perhaps?"

"You are being difficult, Holmes."

She huffed at him. "I am not trying to be. Not this time, I assure you. I am simply trying to keep my friend safe. And the only way to do that is to play your game. And to play, I must write my notes."

He grumbled, but shuffled away to find her a new writing utensil. As soon as his back was turned, she quietly ripped the paper with Eddy's number and slipped it under the napkin. If she could get this to the maid, who could ring Scotland Yard, then they'd be rescued.

Dearborn returned with a pencil and settled back in his seat.

Beside Irene, Joe swayed back and forth, his fingers twitching in his lap. He was coming to, but his eyes were still glassy. If she could get him to eat, that would help clear the drugs from his system.

Dearborn spoke as excitedly as ever, as if he hadn't just murdered two people and were holding Irene and Joe hostage.

"So now that we have the evidence there is a hound, what do you think this could mean? And what of the convict? Could this be our dead man?"

Irene glanced at Joe, but he didn't seem to hear.

"Perhaps the hound… belongs to the convict," she tried but their host shook his head.

"No, Miss Holmes. Please follow the story."

"I don't know the story."

His lip curled in disgust. "You haven't read your own father's work? What kind of a daughter are you?"

As much as she tried not to let this man get to her, the task was becoming more difficult. She was challenging him and he was fighting back. She had to remember that this man was a lunatic. Psychotic. And didn't truly care about her or her father.

If Joe were coherent, he'd say something along the lines of not riling this man up. He was dangerous. They were on the outskirts of any decently sized town and far from help.

She had to keep playing his game. Had to keep him calm and force his guard down, so she could run at the first possible chance.

"What happens after we solve the mystery," she asked, picking at her lunch. "Will you simply let us go?"

Dearborn ripped a large chunk of chicken from the leg. "When everything is done, and I have picked your brain to its fullest extent, you and Dr. Watson are more than welcome to walk right out the front door."

"With a bullet following us, no doubt."

Dammit, Irene. She needed to curtail her snide remarks. This was much more difficult than she'd imagined. Usually, she had Joe to squeeze her hand or knock her knee and bring her down.

Dearborn sighed. "Miss Holmes, my goal is to show the world that Sherlock Holmes is the greatest man to ever live. That everyone must come to love him as I do. Once I convince you that I can do that, then you won't want to leave. You will want to help spread the word about Dr Watson's stories and share your own part of the tales."

"You are now speaking about the stories as if they are the Bible."

"They are! Look, Miss Holmes, I know your father would want—"

"You're psychotic," she snapped.

Joe finally reacted beside her, squeezing her hand. But she couldn't stop.

"My father wouldn't even give you the time of day, let alone any thought. I do not want to play your little game anymore. Let us—"

The click of a revolver cut her words off. Morris stood behind Joe, the barrel pointed at the back of his head. Though still drugged, he was aware enough to freeze as the metal pressed against his head.

Dearborn sighed. "You both are staying right here. Now, pick up your fork and finish your meal. We will take a small break from the story to calm down."

Irene wanted to spew a thousand insults at him and fling a knife right between his eyes. But she could do nothing with a gun against Joe's head. Dearborn knew he had her. Joe was becoming expendable. Her promise to cooperate was the only thing keeping him alive. To think what would happen if this lunatic didn't care how unruly she became churned her stomach.

She stared him down as she picked up her fork and waited. Dearborn motioned for Morris to step back, and as soon as he did, Irene began to eat.

Once she figured out how to get out of this situation, Dearborn wasn't making it off this property.

Chapter VIII
Yet Another Body

Joe shook his head again, his mind becoming clearer as the afternoon went on. He was sore. His mouth felt like cotton. However, he wasn't as drugged as he knew he should be. The butler surely made a mistake with the dosing. For someone as slender as Joe, it took a lot of medicine to make him dozy. He picked up the chicken leg and started eating. The food would and drink would clear the effects of the drug as well.

He would still need to act as though he was dozy, lest they top up the medication. He slowed his eating slightly, but he already felt much clearer in his head. The world still sounded as if under water, but he could hear every word spoken in the conversation between Irene and Dearborn.

Thus, Joe pieced together the middle of the day.

He'd seen Irene write a note, though he wasn't sure what it would say. They were all still playing this silly mystery game. And two men had been murdered. Their wives were nowhere to be seen. Joe wouldn't be surprised if Dearborn had ordered them dead as well.

He looked at Irene. It took a good few seconds for her face to become clear as she ate her lunch. His ribs clawed at his lungs and he instantly wanted to hug her.

Irene was shaken. It was rare to see her truly fearful, but in this moment, with her white knuckles and clenched fists, she was ready to either murder everyone in the room or break down.

As they finished their meal, Dearborn nattered on about needing to investigate more outside. Joe tuned him out, trying to act dozy enough so they wouldn't sedate him again. He'd almost finished his meal when Irene's words caught his attention.

"Another body?"

"That's the rumour," Dearborn exclaimed.

"Yes, I suppose we should see it."

Joe tried to figure out who was left to murder and he only thought of the two women.

Irene and Dearborn stood. Irene helped him to his feet as well, and stars flew around his vision. He leaned on the table to steady himself as she wrapped her arm through his. They followed Dearborn outside once again. Morris followed behind, the gun no doubt pointed at them still. Joe leaned on Irene, but didn't apply all his weight. He did his best to stay stumbly and groggy, and hoped Irene got the message.

They all traipsed down to the stone huts again. The fresh air was doing wonders for Joe, and by the time they got to their destination, he simply felt like he'd had a few too many drinks the night before.

Just as Dearborn said, there was another body. Joe hadn't seen him before, and there wasn't any fanfare to this death. He was shot. The original story didn't even have another body, did it? Surely not one that wasn't simply executed. He tried to pull the details of the tale to the forefront, but as clear as his mind was now, there were parts that were still exceptionally cloudy.

Irene crouched and poked around the victim. She peeked at the man's ear and pulled away a bit of his curled hair. A large brown birthmark sat just under the earlobe. Joe had seen that marking before. His partner picked up the man's hand and studied his thumb. He tried to see what she observed, but only saw a shortened nail and dirty hands of someone who worked in the kitchen.

She stood and turned to Joe, ready to narrate. He reached for a bag he did not have, and a notebook that sat up in his pack in the bedroom.

"What is it, Holmes," Dearborn asked.

"I am trying to make notes," she said reluctantly. "But my note-taker is still groggy."

"What about your notebook?"

"I am not used to carrying one, so I have left it inside. No matter—"

"Big matter!" Dearborn cried, flipping back to jovial. "Morris, retrieve Miss Holmes's notebook!"

The butler obliged, heading back to the house.

Now was their chance. Joe had no idea what Irene was planning, and Dearborn had a pistol on him, but it was two against one. He wasn't sure how well he could fight – and he didn't think he could run in a perfectly straight line – but if she decided to bolt, he'd follow directly behind her.

"Is this why Mary is complying?" Irene asked Dearborn. "Because you've threatened her brother? Does she know he's dead? Also, that butler of yours – clearly, he is an American Marine. So why does he listen to you? What debt does he owe you?"

Joe stared at her. Why didn't she run? Was he missing something? Had her desire to solve this second mystery overpowered her need to escape?

Dearborn sighed. "We are getting off topic, Miss Holmes."

Irene opened her mouth to answer, but a door slamming at the house cut her off. Morris strode toward them.

"Mary," he said in his rough American accent. "She was telephoning the police. I think I stopped her before the call went through."

"You *think* you stopped her?" Dearborn roared.

"She wasn't speaking to anyone, but she told me she was trying to telephone the police."

Joe stepped right beside Irene. They could try to run now, but with Morris here, they wouldn't make it too far. And there was no way they were fighting both of them off.

And god knows what Morris did to that poor maid.

Dearborn's neck reddened; it crept up into his cheeks.

"Why does no one want to play my game? It's not that hard. Follow along, and we can all have fun. We can all be in Sherlock Holmes' world!"

Irene clenched her fists. Joe grabbed her arm. She was about to do something dangerous and his reflexes and mind weren't quite up to snuff yet.

"We *are* in his world," she bit out. "He isn't a fictional—"

"Shut up! You have been nothing but a selfish, worthless, little girl the whole time you've been here. You were supposed to be like him, but you are not."

He aimed the gun at them.

Joe tried to tug Irene away but she stood firm.

"Are you really going to shoot Sherlock Holmes' daughter? Is that the legacy you want to leave?"

Dearborn yelled in his rage and Joe held Irene tighter. He wasn't sure what he could do from behind her, but he needed to get her out of the way of the gun.

Dearborn pressed his palm into his forehead. "The game is done! Finished! You are horrible and uncooperative. Even your father would've obeyed more than this. I am going to dig out everything on Sherlock Holmes, and you are going to tell me *everything* you know about him. And if you so much as whisper a curse word at me, I will kill Dr. Watson and make you watch every second of him bleed out. Now, I need time to think. To the cellar, both of you."

Irene didn't move.

Joe tensed. He still held her arm, giving it a small tug. Dearborn had lost it, wholly and completely, and he was bound to shoot them out of pure frustration. If Joe could get Irene safely to the cellar, then they could discuss how to get out of this.

Thankfully, though, Irene finally cooperated. She latched onto Joe and together they marched back toward the house at gunpoint.

The cellar was beside the kitchen. Morris opened the door and they descended into the cold room. There were posts throughout, holding up the house, and the floor was dirt. It was cold and dark, except for a few lanterns lit – presumably so the cook could see as he gathered vegetables for the meals.

The cook who was now dead.

As well as the two other men. Perhaps their wives as well.

Joe's stomach churned.

Dearborn came down the small stairs, pointing his gun. Joe's heart thudded loud in his ears.

Had Dearborn changed his mind? Was he going to kill them? Did the maid get through to Scotland Yard? Was *she* dead?

His ribs squeezed his lungs again. He tried to breathe through the panic. Images flashed in his brain. Bombs. Screams. Bound in a wagon. Horses crying. He hadn't had a true flashback like this in ages. He coughed and leaned against the pole as the butler came toward him, a pile of ropes in his hands.

Chapter IX

A Confession and an Escape

Irene's throat was dry. Her heart raced, and her ears burned with anger. She wanted to kill them both where they stood.

Joe coughed behind her. He was panicking again. She needed to go to him, but Morris stood between the pair. He tried to bind Joe's hands, but her friend squirmed and rolled away.

She needed to get him out of here. She should've taken the chance out in the garden. She had no idea how far they would've gotten before Morris caught up to them, but she should've tried.

What was left to do? Reason with Dearborn? Could he even be reasoned with?

"Release us," she tried. "Send us back to London, and you shall never hear from us again. No one would believe our story anyway. I can't even remember the names of the people you've murdered."

The man considered her offer for a mere second before bursting out in a maniacal laugh.

"I have the daughter of Sherlock Holmes in my grasp. You are not going anywhere. All I wanted to do was play a simple game, but you have ruined that. So, now I must think of another way to use you to your fullest potential."

Morris started on her hands, wrapping them in ropes as she stared down Dearborn. He sighed and shook his head, continuing his monologue:

"I must admit, I am disappointed in you. Sherlock Holmes would never have put himself in such a situation. I wasn't going to hold you to the same standards, obviously. You may be of his blood, but you are still a woman and… Well, not Sherlock. I will be back when I've figured out what story we want to play. Perhaps *The Solitary Cyclist*? Or *The Speckled Band*? I'm sure there is a snake I can find somewhere. Or maybe I'll force you to tell me about him like I threatened in the garden. That might be more fun."

She should've kept silent and let this lunatic walk away. She should've tended to Joe and figured out a way to escape once Dearborn and Morris had left them.

But she didn't.

Instead, she snapped at him.

"I will stay in here until I rot before I participate in the farce that is your life. You are pathetic. If my father ever met you, he would be disgusted. You are a psychotic madman attempting to live out some delusion because you have nothing of value in your own life. I don't even feel pity for you, because that would mean there is something inside you to be helped or redeemed—"

He grabbed Irene's throat before she could react. His fingers squeezed her neck, cutting off her air. Her bound hands tried to push him off, but to no avail.

Behind her, Joe cried her name. He was a blur as he collided with Dearborn. They both fell to the ground as Irene stumbled back, catching her breath.

Morris grabbed Joe, throwing him to the side. He punched him in the stomach once, then twice. Joe keeled over, coughing and spluttering, bound hands over his head, blocking his face. Irene started toward them, ready to fight Morris to the death but Dearborn stepped in her way. She kicked him in the groin, then shouldered him aside. With her bound hands, she was limited, but not wholly incompetent.

She launched her body into Morris's, sending the man flying. She fell to her hands and knees overtop of Joe, remaining there.

He curled under her, still breathing hard, his hands digging into his hair.

The butler rolled to his feet and looked at her. She stared back. Sweat dotted her forehead and a bead rolled down her back, but she would die before she let him touch Joe again. She was finished with everything. She simply wanted to make good on her promise to see both these men put in the ground.

Dearborn snapped at Morris, "Leave them."

The butler obeyed. Giving Irene one final glare, he walked away. She turned to face Dearborn. His nose was bloody and his eyes red-rimmed from her kick.

He thrust a finger at her. "You want to be as clever as Sherlock Holmes? Figure a way out of this one."

He marched up the stairs and slammed the door. She heard a padlock click and she finally took a breath. Then she crawled off of Joe and stroked his hair.

"They're gone. You're okay, Joe."

He let out a ragged breath, but stayed curled against her. She scooped him up as best she could and wiggled beneath him. Placing his head in her lap, she hugged his shoulders and pressed her forehead into his hair.

"You're okay. You're safe. I'm safe."

Irene repeated the words over and over until his breathing calmed. She lifted her head, sitting straight, as a tear rolled down her cheek. She was sore. Joe was hurt. They were trapped. They were both scared.

She'd failed this one. Not like the previous cases where she had been just frustrated that she'd lost the mystery. This was a true failure.

She'd been so insistent on earning money that she didn't wait for Joe before accepting this case. And she'd been so stubborn about proving she knew her father better than this man. She'd kept playing his game instead of getting both her and Joe out.

But they were here. And she needed to figure out how to get them out safe. Or at least get Joe out.

He didn't deserve to be hurt because he was protecting her. He didn't deserve to have another panicked episode, having flashbacks to a horrid war. All because of her.

She wasn't worth it.

Joe sniffled and sat up slowly. He moved back beside her, placing his head on her shoulder. His breathing had calmed but he still shivered. Another tear escaped her eyes, then another. Irene tried to blink them away, but to no avail. This cellar was cold, they were both sore, and she truly didn't know if they would make it out.

Her best friend in the whole world had to endure one of his episodes that he hadn't had in almost a year. He was beaten, and bound, all because of her.

She opened her mouth but all that came out was a squeak. Clearing her throat, she tried again.

"I am sorry, Joe." Her voice was weak, but in the cold stale air of the cellar, it seems to echo off the walls.

He shifted beside her, sitting straight and wincing. "For what?"

She quickly wiped her tears, no doubt spreading dirt across her cheeks. She kept her head down and poked at the hard ground.

"For all the trouble I get us into. Both of us have gotten more scrapes and bumps in the past two years than at any point during the war. And voluntarily, too. Why? Because I *am* trying to be my father? I'm trying to prove I am as good as him? There is no point. It is so ridiculous."

"There is no point in what?"

She refused to look at him, but felt his stare boring into her. His soft blue-eyed gaze would only make her feel worse.

"Any of this. Do we truly help people? Or are we simply fulfilling some fantasy to be useful, just like this man is doing with his Sherlock Holmes delusion? The work you do at the vet, and the consulting I used to do for Eddy, helped London more than anything we're doing right now."

Joe was silent. Fresh tears started in her eyes. He agreed with her. He knew what she meant and had probably thought the same multiple times before. If they ever made it out of here, they'd go back to what they were doing before the war and be safer for it.

"That is simply untrue," he said finally, the soothing tone in his voice turning stern. "While we may not have swiped people from moving trains, or rescued them as they fell from rooftops, we've stopped many plans before they got to the point of hurting people. Remember the young couple in love? The Spaniard and the rich daughter? We saved them. We also saved those young women from the man lobotomising them, and probably saved more young women from his clutches. We've even saved film stars, and animals, from certain death or punishment. We have done well, Irene. We've made a difference."

Of course she remembered all the cases. Even the ones that shouldn't have been. She sighed, still staring down at the dirt.

"But there have been cases that shouldn't have been touched. And I am truly sorry to have put you in danger all for my stupid pride."

"Do you think I would've come along if I didn't want to?"

He wasn't understanding, and he needed to. She wasn't sure exactly what she was trying to say, but he simply wasn't understanding. She stood abruptly, needing to pace. As she did, she worked on the rope wrapped around her wrists.

"Of course you would've come along. Because that is what you do. You risk your life and do things that make you uncomfortable all to appease me. And what do I give you in return? Frustration? A certain anxiety? The inability to relax when we are outside Baker Street? I don't even understand why you aid me. I have not earned your loyalty, Joe. I have not earned your friendship."

He used the post behind him to get to his feet, wincing the whole time. Irene tried not to watch as she paced. She'd almost freed herself though, working the layers of rope up and around her thumb and off her fingers.

"Then why have I stayed with you at Baker Street for almost two years?"

She shrugged, turning snippy. "You needed a place to live. I got you a dog. The close proximity to one another left you with a false sense of need. I am trying not to sound pitiful, or ask you to tell me why I am such a brilliant flatmate, I promise. And I am not trying to wallow. I am simply trying to understand.

You could've left to be with Sarah. Could've afforded another flat, all to yourself, with a large bedroom and a kitchen and no silly experiments or papers anywhere."

"You're right."

Irene froze, finally looking at him. She knew it, her dearest friend was realising what a waste of a life he'd had.

He leaned on the post, clearly in pain. "I could have all those things, but you wouldn't be there. I wouldn't eat breakfast with you every morning. I wouldn't read you my favourite novels every night. I wouldn't have Isla or Miss Hudson. I wouldn't have learnt all the things you've taught me. I wouldn't have had any of the adventures we've been on, or become friends with Lestrade."

"You wouldn't get frustrated with me though," she said. "You wouldn't need to go for walks because I have done something to anger you. You wouldn't need to double check what was in containers in the refrigerator before opening them."

He shrugged and smiled at her, bruising eyes crinkling. It was the smile he saved just for her. She was starting to understand what it meant and it made her squirm. Mostly because she didn't know if she ever smiled at him that way.

"All of that just comes with the Irene Holmes package. I'm not allowed to have any of the laughs, the silly conversations or the wild adventures, without an exhausted sigh, or an eye roll every now and then."

She snorted and finally got free of the ropes. "Trapped in a cellar of a madman is a bit more than a tired sigh."

"Sometimes your friendship comes with a life-threatening evening or two. So be it."

She played with the rope still in her hands, staring once again at the ground. Maybe Joe really meant what he said. Perhaps he did truly love life at Baker Street. He'd never lied to her before, especially about his feelings towards things.

"You're serious, aren't you?"

She looked at him again, prepared for a crinkly-eyed smile or an exasperated eye roll. Instead, he looked upon her as if studying a painting at a museum, or reading a book he was all-enthralled with.

He pushed himself off the post and closed the small gap between them. She thought he might take her hands, but instead, his bound wrists found her face. He tucked her short hair behind her ears, then cupped her cheeks in his hands. His pupils were still dilated from either the drugs or the dim light. The warmth from his body radiated through her clothes.

She felt tears start all over again. She hated crying, especially if she didn't even know why. And she had no idea why a tear made its way down her cheek. Joe swiped it with his thumb, then pressed his lips to her forehead.

"I am serious, because I..." he trailed off, peering down at her, a million thoughts behind his eyes. If he was going to say anything, it was lost.

Instead he lifted his bound arms over her head and pulled her into him, squishing her face into his chest.

"I would not trade all the luxury goods or stable income in the world if it meant losing you."

Even more tears started. Irene tried to stop them, but they seeped into his shirt.

He had such faith in her, and every time she got him injured. How can he believe in her this much? How could he keep trusting her? He claimed that he enjoyed their friendship, but was he lying? Was he delusional? Surely not.

Her confidence and self-assuredness had never been a problem, and she couldn't care less what others thought of her, but as the past two years went on, she found herself worried about what Joe would think. She thought about him often; most of the time she considered him when acting upon any decisions. The most recent cases had been poor examples of this, but she had been worried about his feelings. This meant she cared. He was her best friend. A member of the family. She loved him.

She was *in* love with him.

No, that wasn't it. She hadn't allowed herself to be in love with him. Besides, that's not what they had between them. And what good would being in love with Joe do for her? Nothing but heartbreak. Joe wasn't with her. He didn't want to be in love with her. She wouldn't know what to do with him even if she was in love with him.

She buried her face deeper into his chest and hugged him tighter.

"Irene?"

"Hm?"

"When did you free your hands?"

"As I was pacing. I have fat wrists and narrow hands. Morris wasn't paying attention and I kept them apart enough to slip my hands out."

"Ah."

He kept hold of her, obviously not wanting to let her go. And a part of her didn't want him to. But she had to figure out how to get them out of this mess. Dearborn said he was going to pull out all the items and articles he had on her father so she could tell him more. The thought of that make her stomach flip and she felt sick. But perhaps that was the only choice. Maybe she had to face the madman and tell him anecdotes to soothe his madness. Feed into the obsession until she found a way out.

But how to keep Joe safe in the process?

What would her father do?

He'd fake his own death to keep his loved ones safe. He'd disappear into opium dens and not tell Uncle John so he'd stay away from the danger. He'd leave his friend somewhere safe until he could bring Uncle John with him – or return to him in one piece.

Keeping Joe safe meant keeping him in this cellar until she could deal with Dearborn and come back for him. If Joe was out there with her, he would be collateral.

She had to truly hope that the maid had called Eddy. If not, she had to let her escape so she could get a hold of someone – if she was still alive.

And she had to decommission the butler. If it was just her and Dearborn, she could win. She could outsmart him, and if he figured her out, she could overpower him.

But Joe had to stay here. He wasn't going to like that option very much.

As comfortable and safe as she felt against his body, she had to leave. She broke away and he lifted his arms over hear head.

"You okay?"

She nodded, refusing to look at him in case his puppy-dog eyes caused her to second guess her plan. She gripped the rope tight in her hands.

"I am sorry, Joe."

"You don't need to apologize, Irene."

"I do. Because you aren't going to like this."

She looped the rope around his bound hands and tugged hard toward the wooden post in the middle of the room. Joe stumbled and nearly fell, but managed to stay on his feet. She wrapped her rope around the pole multiple times and secured it with every knot she knew.

"Irene? What are you doing?"

She tied the last knot and stepped away. "I am saving us."

"What?" He tugged at the rope. "No, Irene. Whatever it is, we can do it together."

"Not this time."

"Irene—"

Now that Joe was tied up, and it was time for her to leave, panic gripped her chest. Bile rose in her throat. What if she didn't make it back? What if they were separated for longer than she planned? All the feelings that bounced in her head wanted to come out. Her thoughts about her friendship with Joe were on the tip of her tongue, begging her to speak. It almost made her sick all over again. Was she about to confess her feelings like some love-struck heroine from the films? Or was she a dying woman making her last confession?

"Irene!" Joe's voice snapped her back to the cellar.

"Listen to me, Joe."

"Untie me and we can figure it out—"

"I already have. You must stay here. Now, please listen."

"Untie me—"

"Doctor, please! Shut up and let me speak. If you get to say all those nice things about me, then I get to say something nice to you."

"Irene—"

She averted her gaze downward, attempting to speak her feelings. It was unnatural and odd to open those doors but a part of it felt like something she had to do.

"You are invaluable to me. If I hadn't met you, I would've been lonely and sad and miserable. You made my life better. You made *me* better. I do believe I love you, Joe Watson, though I am not sure how and in what way. It is different than how I love Eddy and Miss Hudson, but it is just as great. I do not know what it means, but it makes us special."

She looked at him and wished she hadn't. Tears welled in his eyes, his shoulders slumped, and he didn't fight the restraints.

"Irene…" His voice was barely above a whisper. "Please don't leave."

Before she could change her mind, she pivoted and headed for the cellar door. She banged on the wood as loud as she could.

"Dearborn! I will tell you what you want to know! Dearborn!"

She heard Joe strain against the rope. "Irene, no! They'll kill you!"

"I'll come back for you once they are taken care of."

"No!" His voice wavered as he held back his tears. "We can figure this out together."

She banged on the door again, ignoring him.

"Dammit, Irene," he kicked at the dirt. "You cannot say you love someone, then run away into danger!"

"Yes, I can, if it keeps that person alive."

She went to bang again, but a key turned in the lock. Suddenly, Dearborn was leering down at her.

"What are you doing? How are you free?"

She ignored his questions. "I will talk to you about my father."

"And what of Dr. Watson?"

"He is staying where he is. And the longer he remains safe, the more I will speak with you about whatever you want to know. Maybe it's time to tell my side of Sherlock Holmes' stories."

He regarded her and it took all her willpower to not punch him in the face again. She tried to look earnest, truthful and defeated.

It must've worked, because he stepped to the side and let her pass.

As she climbed the stairs, Joe yelled after them. "If you hurt her, I'll kill you—"

Dearborn slammed the cellar door.

"Oh dear," he said, securing the lock. "He seems quite upset."

"He does not want me to be up here. But, if any harm comes to Joe, I will do everything in my power to make sure neither you, nor your butler see the light of day again. Furthermore, I will have a story printed about how awful you were and I will convince my father that you are nothing more than a maggot. He will know your name only to spit on it. Do you understand?"

His eye twitched. "Then why call on me?"

"I am intrigued, I confess. Unwillingly so, but intrigued, nonetheless. You have things of my father that not even I have seen, nor do know about. Perhaps a discussion about him is warranted."

He rose a brow, sceptical on her sudden change of heart, no doubt. But the offer was too good for him to pass up.

"Fine. Follow me, Miss Holmes."

She trailed behind Dearborn toward the study.

"Those two men you murdered—" she started, but he cut her off.

"They died for the game!"

"Yes, for the game. The one outbid you on a house—"

"A famous house!"

"Yes. And the other one… Something to do with his wife."

"She was supposed to be mine. We went steady for a while until she decided to be with him."

"And that was enough to kill them?"

"Of course!"

Irene had no further questions; she was too bewildered.

And they had come to the study.

Laid all over the room were the articles and objects from the forbidden east wing. Dearborn stood in the middle of them, stupid jovial smile on his face once again.

Irene gazed at the items, seeing articles and old photographs of her father, Uncle John, and even of Nana Hudson, the housekeeper who tended to Father before Irene's own Miss Hudson. These were all photographs and articles she could probably find stashed away at her father's farm. She had a plan to look at them eventually, but on her time and on her own terms. Not forced upon her, like the impromptu psychiatry session during their lobotomy case.

Morris stomped into the room, heading straight for his master. Irene ignored them as she lifted an article from the table. It proclaimed Sherlock Holmes dead. She stared at the headline, then spotted the other article she'd gleaned while in the east wing. The photograph attached was grainy, but it was unmistakably her father strolling down Baker Street, a little girl in tow. The article went on to state that despite not taking clients anymore, Sherlock Holmes was still active in London with who appears to be his daughter. It left off asking the question, "Is she the next great Holmes?"

Irene had no idea who could've taken the photograph, or cared enough to send it to a newspaper. Unless this was Dearborn all along, submitting articles and photos all to keep up with the story.

From behind her, the man let out a great sigh. "Oh, Miss Holmes. I suppose I should expect nothing less."

She rolled her eyes, turning to him while suppressing a curse, article still in her hand. What was his problem now?

Dearborn held the napkin with Eddie's telephone number. "Mary has informed us that she did connect with this number."

He sauntered toward her. She quickly looked over to Morris. His knuckles on one fist were bloody.

He stayed at the door while Dearborn continued toward Irene. He peered down at the note, a crooked, heinous smile on his face.

"This excites me greatly, Miss Holmes. To see DI Lestrade's name written down is such a thrill. Tell me, this is not the DI from the stories, is it? It can't be as he must be long retired by now. Is this his son? Oh, how amazing! Both generations communicating with each other. He must be one of the DIs from the photographs I have of you. Now, would he be the dapper dresser? Or the taller gentleman?"

Irene shoved the article in her pocket, freeing her hands.

Dearborn circled her, continuing his monologue. "Regardless, this will not do. See, now you've put all this in danger. As much as I would love to wait for DI Lestrade to show up, I believe he will bring other constables, and Morris and I are simply no match for them. All I wanted was for you and I to talk. But that is ruined.

"I did not want to kill you. But perhaps that is what's needed. I mean, I could simply leave, but I do believe you will find me, should you be free."

Irene's heart raced, but she tried to remain calm. As long as they were both here, she could deal with them. As long as they didn't go after Joe. This was the exact reason she needed to be here by herself. They might've killed her partner already had he been in this room.

Dearborn paced and sighed, clasping his hands together dramatically. "Perhaps I am not meant to be a friend to the Holmes family. Perhaps I am meant to be a Moriarty. A villain."

Irene did her best to hide her laughter. Sweat appeared on her forehead again as her nerves fired. "You are psychotic."

He ignored her, still pacing, and speaking as if to an audience, and yet to no one. "Perhaps my legacy is to be the one who killed Sherlock Holmes' daughter. Fulfil the circle that Moriarty could not complete."

Irene snorted. "You are not my Moriarty. I already met and defeated her. You are simply a man."

She needed to stop talking. Her mouth would get her in trouble or killed.

Or even worse: get Joe killed.

She also needed to escape. That would require all her cleverness and bravery. There was no way this was the end of her.

She needed to see Joe again.

She needed to see her father.

Dearborn kept monologuing, wandering around the room, but Irene wasn't paying attention. Morris still blocked the door. She'd either have to defeat him, or reel him in to escape. She looked around the room for things to use as Dearborn droned on.

The fireplace poker to stab and swipe.

Dirt from her shoes to be thrown in eyes.

And one of them had a gun. But who?

Dearborn had the revolver and loaded bullets into the chamber. She bit back a smile, thrilled that the less capable man had the weapon she needed.

"I am sorry, Miss Holmes."

"So am I." She puffed out her chest, bravado and confidence growing. "For stealing away the chance of you leaving a legacy. I promised you everyone would know your name as a maggot squirming across the earth, and I intend to keep that promise."

Chapter X

The End of Baskerville

Joe stared at the closed cellar door, shaking, sweating, ready to vomit.

Irene left.

She'd walked out right into the clutches of that madman.

And he'd let her go.

"I do believe I love you, Joe Watson."

The rest of her words played back in his mind as jumbled sentences. His nerves fired too rapidly to make sense of everything she said. But he knew that she loved him.

He pulled at the ropes, but it was useless. Letting out a yell, he kicked at the wooden pole, but all it did was topple him over. The rope had just enough slack to allow him to reach the knots on the other side. If he could loosen those, he'd be free.

As soon as he spotted the mess that was behind the pole, Joe groaned. A dozen knots – each one different – tied in a stack. His hands shook. His vision was still blurry from the sweat, the tears and the last of the drugs wearing off.

But he had to try.

He worked the rope, breathing deep, calling upon years of performing surgery on animals to keep his hands steady. Despite the chilly air, sweat rolled down his face and a bead dropped in his eye. He blinked it away and kept at the knots. One after another, they unravelled. As soon as the ropes came undone, Joe stumbled back, coughing, hand clutching his chest. His wrists were still bound from Dearborn, but at least he could move around.

There was nothing of use in the cellar except a table of old pots and pans, and a few crates of potatoes. He tipped them over, spilling the vegetables, hoping for something of use. Then, in the last crate was a dull peeling knife. He flipped it in his grasp and awkwardly sliced at the ropes until his wrists were free.

He breathed deep in relief and smelled smoke.

Fire.

Coming from the house above.

Snapping curse words at the empty air, he rushed to the door. He'd heard Dearborn lock it earlier, but he shouldered the wood anyway. It groaned but didn't budge. He took a run at it, hoping to pop the door off the old hinges, but he crashed into it instead, nearly dislocating his shoulder.

There had to be another way.

The smell of smoke grew as he scrambled for some sort of tool. In the corner of the room were two old extra bricks. He swiped one and made for the door again, smashing one brick into the hinge. It bounced off the metal, but the wood creaked.

Joe hit the hinge again. Then again. And again, crying out with each contact. His hands warmed with blood as the brick dug into his skin. The metal bent, but his arms were like jelly. He only had a few more hits in him.

A gunshot rang through the house and echoed down to the cellar.

Joe gasped, chocking on the smoke.

Irene.

With a mighty cry of anger, he took one final swing. The hinge popped off, the wood splintering beneath it. Throwing the brick to the floor, he pushed the door open and ran for it.

Smoked billowed down into the cellar. Joe pulled his shirt over his mouth and nose. He hurried through the kitchen and through the dining room to the hallway. The fire came from the study, seemingly contained in the room. Something shiny splattered in the hallway, and a fire poker lay in the middle of the puddle.

A pair of legs stuck out from the sitting room. A woman's legs, wearing boots. Not moving. Despite the fire blazing through the house, Joe's blood went ice cold. He stared at the feet, willing his own to move him forward. Were they Irene's?

She did wear boots like these, he was sure.

Which meant…

Dearborn stumbled out of the room, cut and bloodied, but alive. He tripped over the feet, scowled, and kicked the leg.

As if looking through a telescope, or a sniper rifle, Joe's vision tunnelled to the maniac.

He was alive.

He was escaping.

No.

Joe ran through the smoke, over the slick floor. He grabbed Dearborn's shoulders and slammed him into the wall. His nose was broken. Joe punched it anyway and Dearborn's head smacked against the wall.

Joe hit him again.

The man collapsed, obviously dizzy. Joe went down with him, slipping on the bloodied floor. He knelt on Dearborn's gut, causing him to cough and splutter. Joe hit him over and over, in the face, in the chest, wherever his fist could land. A rib cracked under his knee. He leaned forward, putting even more weight on that spot. Another rib snapped. His hand was numb and slipped on what was left of Dearborn's face.

Tears flooded his eyes and everything blurred.

He wasn't even sure what he was hitting any more.

"Joe!"

That voice. Impossible.

Irene was laying on the ground dead.

"Joe!"

Her voice again, floating through the smoke.

Hands grabbed his arms, dragging him off Dearborn. He spun, knocking them away. A body stood amongst the dying smoke. He leapt at the person, shoving them against the wall, blinking way tears and sweat and smoke. His arm pressed into the person's throat, pinning them to the wall.

"Joe, it's *me*! Irene!"

Hearing her name forced everything into focus.

He was choking her. She clawed his arm to release herself.

He gasped and scrambled back, tripping over Dearborn's body. He fell to the ground.

Irene coughed and rubbed her neck. "We have to go. The fire's out, but we have to get away from the smoke."

She had a cut on her face and her shirt sleeve was ripped.

But she was alive.

Slowly, things clicked into place. His leg still rested on Dearborn and a part of him didn't even want to look at the man. He laid in the hallway, blood pooling under him, face unrecognisable.

Bile rose in Joe's throat.

"Did I…" He couldn't say it. "Did I kill him?"

Irene stared for a second, then crouched to their deranged host. She checked for a pulse. Joe felt pale, sick, ready to collapse. He had beat a man to death with his own hands.

Irene pulled a revolver from her waistband, aimed and shot.

The body jerked.

"I killed him. Do you hear me, Joe? You left him alive and I killed him."

Her voice was garbled and still a bit muffled, but he nodded. He understood. Though his gut told him different.

But Irene wouldn't shoot a dead man just to appease him. She wouldn't waste a bullet like that.

Which meant he made *her* kill the man. He should've done it. He should've finished Dearborn off.

"Joe, we need to leave."

He stood shakily, his hearing restored, the fog in his brain clearing. He took one last look at what was left of Dearborn. Then he looked at Irene.

She was alive. And she was holding on to him.

He'd escaped the cellar to save her. It was time to follow through.

He grasped her hand, leading them toward the front door. He didn't stop running, nor did he let go of her, until they pushed through the door. They collapsed on the cold grass and Joe still refused to let go of her hand.

Sirens sounded in the distance, cutting through the hgaze and smoke filling the night air.

He looked at Irene, finally able to see her clearly. She coughed and favoured the arm he wasn't holding on to. He pulled her into him, pressing her into his chest. She squirmed, but he held tight.

"I'm fine, Joe," she said, still coughing into his shirt. But Joe only tightened his grip. She sighed and curled into his lap, clinging to his shirt. "Alright, maybe I'm not fine."

He didn't know what to say to her. He was afraid to talk in case he started coughing. So, he simply held her against him.

Lestrade and half a dozen police cars surrounded the house. The DI shouted orders, then spotted the pair under the window. He rushed to them and dropped to his knees.

"My god, what happened? Where's all this blood coming from?"

Irene extricated herself from Joe's lap, but he still refused to release her hand. They both stood as she spoke.

"There are two women in there, still alive. As well as bodies out the back garden, and two in the house. And a dead maid—"

"We need to go to the hospital," Joe interrupted. The constables could find the bodies easily enough – it was their job after all. Irene was hurt and needed help, and that was his top priority.

"You certainly do," Lestrade agreed.

"Can you or one of your constables drive us to the nearest one?"

"Of course. I can take your statements in the car. I brought the whole cavalry, including Gregory. Let me make sure he's secured the scene and we'll go."

"First," Irene said, trying to wriggle out of Joe's grasp. "I can show you—"

"*Hospital* first," Joe said.

Lestrade glanced at her arm. "He's right. You were shot, Irene. It needs to get looked at."

"It's just a scrape."

Joe stared at her. She was *shot*? How could he not have noticed? He needed to get her out of here. She kept coughing as well, the smoke no doubt doing terrible damage to her lungs.

If he didn't take her now, she'd wander back through the whole house again, commanding the constables.

Irene was still arguing with Lestrade, but even in the darkening light, she was pale and shaking. Though Joe's hands were numb, his arms screamed at him, and he was pretty sure he had a broken finger or two, he still scooped her up. She squealed but he held her tight to his body, clasping his broken hand under her shoulders while his other hand held her legs together. He aimed for Lestrade's police car.

"Lestrade, the door," he commanded.

The DI rushed forward and opened the back passenger door. Joe set Irene in the seat, then shut the car before she could protest.

"Stay," he said to her through the window. Her eyes were the biggest he'd seen them, her mouth hanging open. Surprisingly, she didn't look ready to argue, rather she looked like she'd actually listen to him for once.

He turned to Lestrade. "Our bags are in the third bedroom in the west wing. Like Irene said, there are multiple bodies around the property, but the threat should be gone."

Lestrade lifted Joe's wrist. His fingers were dark purple – two of them very clearly broken – and the blood was sticky, drying and staining his skin.

"I'd hate to see the man on the receiving end of this."

"He doesn't look a man anymore."

Eddy clasped Joe's shoulder. "I'm sorry you both had to go through this. Give me five minutes, then we'll get you both to the hospital."

Joe nodded and climbed into the vehicle next to Irene. The pain was settling into his muscles. His whole body pulsed at different rates, as if each limb had its own heartbeat.

He clasped Irene's hand and she intertwined their fingers.

He hadn't felt rage or loss like this since the war. Since he watched his fellow vets all die around him. Gun shots, grenades, German soldiers. So many things had brought death.

And he'd been furious.

But this anger was different. This loss was different.

He'd survived after the war, but struggling to leave it behind – until Irene came into his life.

And he didn't know if he'd survive if she left.

He'd made promises to himself before to not let her get hurt, to keep an eye on her. But from now on, as far as he was concerned, she was his and he was hers.

He squeezed her hand. She shimmied closer, placing her head on his shoulder. They were both sticky, sweaty, exhausted, covered in other people's blood.

But they were together.

'I do believe I love you, Joe Watson.'

And he loved her too.

Baker Street was their home and he was never leaving her again.

Chapter XI

A Legacy to Leave Behind

Irene never left Joe's sight at the small hospital. Or, rather, he refused to go anywhere without her.

Her arm was easy enough to bandage, and she only needed two stitches for the rest of her injuries. Joe, however, was a bit worse for wear. He had a broken hand, with splinters in various places, and bruising that covered half his body.

As Irene sat out in the waiting room while Joe was getting treated, she rubbed her eyes, fighting to stay awake. It neared midnight and they still had an almost three-hour drive back to London.

It was clear her friend was truly mad at her. He'd scooped her up like she was a doll and tossed her in the vehicle. He'd never been that assertive before, not with her. He'd yelled at her before, begged her not to do things, but never commanded her like that.

He'd held her hand in the car, but hadn't looked at her.

Irene couldn't blame him. She'd left him for his own safety, sure, but if he'd left her, she'd be just as furious.

Once they were both bandaged up, they climbed into a clean police vehicle. A constable handed Irene a box of the articles, photographs and other items they were able to salvage from Baskerville. Both of them fell asleep on the drive home and muttered a sleepy goodnight to Eddy when he pulled in front of 221 Baker Street.

Miss Hudson was up pacing, the worried lines in her forehead deeper than usual. As soon as the pair walked through the door, she flung herself at them.

"Edward rang me and told me what happened! But I didn't realise the state you'd be in!"

A barking Isla danced at their feet. Joe stooped to pet the dog.

"We got a bit hurt," he said to the landlady. "But we are okay. A good sleep is required, but first a cup of tea, if you don't mind, Miss Hudson."

"Of course, dear. You two head on upstairs."

Making a start on the stairs, Joe patted his leg for the dog to follow.

Irene watched after him, frustrated that he was being kind and happy to everyone but her. She trailed upstairs, but Joe continued to his room. He only emerged to take his tea from Miss Hudson.

"I'm taking this upstairs. Goodnight – or rather good morning, Miss Hudson."

"Get some sleep dear," she said, heading back to her own bed.

"Goodnight, Irene," he called over his shoulder.

"Night, Joe."

As she heard his door shut, she sunk to the floor with the dog.

"Oh Isla. I've truly done it now."

The dog's big dark eyes blinked up as she nuzzled Irene's hand.

* * * * *

The sun shone through the windows of 221b. Irene covered her eyes, groaning. Warm dog breath panted up at her, forcing her to sit up. She stretched gingerly, stiff and sore. She'd spent the night on the couch, simply too tired to go to her bed. As she stood, still half asleep, Joe's footsteps descended the stairs. He stepped into the sitting room.

"I'm leaving shortly," he said, voice neutral. "I'll be gone overnight, I'll see you when I get back."

"Of course, you will. I'm not going anywhere."

He stared at her for a moment, then grabbed his jacket and headed to the stairs.

Irene sighed. How could she be such an idiot? He was already cross with her, did she need to have a smart mouth as well?

She hurried after him, catching him at the stairs.

"Joe."

He paused at the bottom of the steps.

"I look forward to seeing you when you come back home."

His stern expression softened slightly, and he opened his mouth to speak, but thought again.

Instead, he gave her a curt nod, then left the building.

* * * * *

She had an extra long bath, scrubbing her hair more than she ever had. Then, she moped for the better part of the morning, her arm stinging every now and then. Eddy was due to come over after lunch to collect her statement about the case now that they'd recovered all the bodies.

Irene wandered down the stairs to see Miss Hudson. She didn't believe the woman could cheer her up, as she didn't quite understand what exactly she was feeling, but at least it'd be a distraction.

Miss Hudson was folding laundry as Irene plunked down on the stool next to her. She didn't even know what to say, but luckily, the landlady spoke first.

"That case a tough one, love? I can only imagine with the state you two returned in."

Irene nodded. "This man was obsessed with Father. He had multiple copies of Uncle John's stories, and photos and articles about Father and my life. Eddy collected it all. I have it upstairs."

"Oh my!" Miss Hudson held up two socks to ensure they matched. "Your uncle's stories caused quite a stir. People would line up outside the paper to get the newest copy."

Irene sighed. "He was beloved."

"Much to his chagrin."

Irene grabbed two different socks out of the basket. "Do you think people would still love my father if they knew his mind was going? If they knew he wasn't the same Sherlock Holmes as in the stories?"

Miss Hudson plucked the socks from her, tossing them back in the basket, then took her hands. "He was never truly that man in the stories. John left out some details, and a quarter of those tales were written after you came along, and you aren't mentioned in a single one. John knew what he was doing. He purposefully created Sherlock Holmes – the character – based very closely on your father. Remember, the world will never know him as well as you did. You are his daughter. No matter what anyone says about him, you are the only thing he cares about."

"And his cases. And you… probably."

Miss Hudson smacked her hand. "So cheeky."

Irene took the two socks back and fiddled with them. She opened her mouth to say the thought she'd been afraid to say out loud since the middle of this case, then hesitated.

She tossed the socks and tried again. "Perhaps then, Sherlock Holmes doesn't belong to me."

"What do you mean, dear?"

"The man from Uncle John's writing. He was my father, of course, but the stories became so much bigger than him. If Dearborn loved the character so much, then there are surely others who are just as fond. Though not as mad. Perhaps they've even written their own stories about him."

Miss Hudson smiled at her. "Your uncle made your father a loveable man. As popular as those film stars. As much as you may dislike it, there is a part of him that belongs to the public. John wanted to tell stories of their friendship, and of the smartest man he knew and loved.

"You are the legacy John and Sherlock left behind. But to the public, it is those stories. And they will outlast you and your children, and even your children's children."

"You really think so?"

Miss Hudson nodded. "It's our job to make sure they do."

Irene rolled the socks into a ball, then unfurled them over and over. Perhaps, instead of avoiding the stories, she should read them. See what the public sees in her uncle's words. She'd been so protective over him, but perhaps she needed to let the stories go. Let the public appreciate them.

Miss Hudson took the socks. "But what do I know? I am just a silly old woman!"

"You know a lot, Miss Hudson. And I appreciate you."

The old woman swatted her knee. "Oh, stop. You're going to make me cry."

Irene snorted. "I was hardly inspiring."

"You were nice and spoke from your heart."

Irene frowned and poked at a pile of towels, not quite ready to leave yet. "Do you know where Joe went?"

Miss Hudson pushed her hand away from the clean laundry. "He said he was going back home, then would visit Sarah. He had something important to speak with her about."

"Something important?"

To Irene's surprise, her stomach gurgled in a strange way.

Miss Hudson shrugged. "Perhaps he is finally proposing. Nothing like the adventures you've both been on in the past year to make you rethink your future."

"Proposing?"

"It would be about time too. A year too late, if you ask me."

Irene stared at the woman. She sounded happy, eager for Joe to propose. Did she know what that meant? Did she truly understand the implications of Joe getting married?

"You want him to leave Baker Street then?" Irene didn't mean to snap, but her words didn't seem to affect Miss Hudson.

"Oh, Heavens no, dear. But if his wish is to be married, and it will make him happy, then I want that for him."

A headache crept across Irene's forehead. She had a few pain pills for her arm, perhaps she would take a double dose and sleep off the rest of the day.

"I don't want him to leave Baker Street."

"I know, Love."

"I don't want him to be married." Irene pouted like a child not getting her way. This whole conversation made her feel too much and her body hurt and she wanted to mope again.

"Now, Irene," Miss Hudson tut-tutted. "You can't control that. There is nothing wrong with Sarah. You two get along just fine. It's Joe's choice. Of course, if I had it my way, the two of you would stay here forever. But that's not up to us. Now take these upstairs."

Irene took the laundry basket and stood. "I preferred your other words of wisdom, about Father."

"You never asked me to comfort you, Love. You only asked for my thoughts." Miss Hudson gave her a sly smile.

Irene turned before she either smiled back or rolled her eyes. She traipsed up the stairs, sore and discouraged. Would Joe really leave 221b? Would he leave London altogether? Move closer to his parents?

What if she made 221b better and enticed him to stay? If she did more chores and kept her area tidy? That may work. She could also do more of the shopping alone, instead of dragging him with her all the time. And Miss Hudson did most of the cooking, but perhaps she should learn so she could cook some of Joe's favourites.

She paused on the upper landing and sighed.

All of those things were the job of a wife. Irene didn't want to be a wife. She simply wanted to keep Joe to herself and at Baker Street.

She thought about leaving the laundry basket on their small dining table, as she usually did, but reconsidered. Perhaps being a better flatmate would keep him here for a *bit* longer – or at least make him be happy with her again.

She continued up to the third floor and into Joe's bedroom. The box of his mother's belongings sat on his bed. She swapped it for the laundry basket, placing the box on the floor. She peered inside despite herself.

The small box with the engagement ring was gone.

She jiggled the box, shifting some of the contents, but the ring was nowhere to be found.

She set the box down harder than she meant to and sat on the bed. As she took Joe's folded clothes from the basket, her stomach filled with rocks.

A strange pang in her chest appeared. Was it heartbreak?

No, that was too dramatic.

Miss Hudson, and everyone else in their life, encouraged Joe month after month to propose. It was the correct thing for him to do in this society, and for Sarah.

It was what Irene expected.

So why did she feel so disheartened and small?

She dumped the rest of the laundry on Joe's bed and tossed the laundry basket behind her. It knocked over the bedside lamp. Scowling at the result of her trying to do house chores, she swiped the item from the floor. She went to set it back on the table, but paused.

The worn copy of *The Hobbit* that they always read together sat next to the bed, with the small blue leather ring box on top of it.

She stared at it as if it would suddenly disappear if she looked away.

Joe hadn't taken it with him. Unless…

She grabbed the box and opened it. The diamond shone at her.

Relief washed through her entire body, her eyes threatening tears. Her knees weakened, so she sat on the bed. She grabbed the book as well, holding both close to her chest.

If Joe wasn't proposing, then he would stay at Baker Street, right? If so, then what was he off doing?

Irene sighed.

Living the life he had outside 221b, of course. But he would still come home, right?

She had no idea anymore.

Regardless, she needed to get on with her own life. Which meant tackling tasks she'd been putting off. She peeked at the ring once more, then set the box and book exactly how they were. Standing with some sense of renewal and purpose, she scooped up the laundry basket and headed down the stairs.

She sat down at her desk and stared at the stationary that hadn't moved at all during their adventure. For almost half an hour, Irene held her pen, trying to figure out a way to start the letter. Perhaps she should start at the beginning, when she met Joe. Or perhaps when she left Father for London? Or maybe after Uncle John died?

Irene almost stood up, ready to forget the whole thing for good, but she forced herself to stay in the chair. Putting the pen to the paper, she started with something simple:

Hello Father,

She could tell him about her favourite case. Or about Isla. Or…

She sighed and settled on a funny story to start.

I must tell you about the time Joe and I went undercover as stove repairmen for a man who was keeping his dead daughter in their attic. He'd hired a maid who looked identical to her!

As she continued writing, she found the letter flowed easier than she'd thought. She rambled on about other mysteries she and Joe had solved, about Isla, about dragging Uncle John's Vauxhall out of storage. Miss Hudson probably told him all of this as it was happening, but Irene wrote it down anyway. She asked him about his bees and his violin, and if he knew what type of soil he had in his garden. As she reached the ninth page of inscription, her vision blurred and a tear fell to the page. She scowled and wiped her face. Now was not the time.

She managed to get through another page before exhaustion crept up and she couldn't stop the tears anymore. Cussing, she wiped her face again and tossed the pen down. She could write him novels about her life and adventures, but if ten pages was what she got right now, it would have to do.

She sat at her desk for a while, waiting for her heart to stop racing, and for the tears to cease. She wasn't crying, not truly. Her body just seemed to need a release of the bottled up emotions pertaining to her father.

And Irene couldn't control it.

Which she hated.

Finally, she stuffed the letter into an envelope and sealed it. She wandered down the stairs, the paper in hand.

Miss Hudson was in the kitchen, taking stock of the pantry. Irene paused at the door, fiddling with the letter. She felt ten again, asking questions she couldn't ask her father or uncle. Or simply needing to talk.

"Um…" She couldn't even say the words, so she held out the envelope. Miss Hudson took it from her. As soon as she saw the name, tears sprang up in her eyes.

"Oh, Love…"

"It's a letter. For Father. It's probably too long but I couldn't stop writing." She laughed awkwardly and blinked, keeping her own tears from falling.

"I can go see him tomorrow."

Irene nodded. "Okay. If it's too long, then—"

"Irene." The older woman touched her shoulder. "It could be a hundred pages, and I would read every single word to him."

She bit her lip to keep the tears at bay. "Okay. Thanks, Miss Hudson."

The landlady tucked the letter into her purse. "Why don't I ring that that fish and chip place and have them bring round two dinners. You can eat with me if you like, or upstairs by yourself. What do you think?"

Irene sniffled, a tear finally escaping. "Yes, please."

Chapter XII
A Dramatic Change for the Future

All three of Joe's sisters spoke over one another at the breakfast table. Alice separated her eggs, not eating them. Eleanor had cleared her plate. And Heather, the oldest of the three women, rolled her eyes. She looked like the younger two: dark blonde hair and dark blue eyes. They all still looked like school children to Joe, even though two of them were grown women.

The table they sat at was large and new, bought with the money Joe sent home every time he and Irene had a case. It was never very much, but it kept his family living well, which eased his mind. His mother had raved about the new refrigerator they'd received on sale, as well as her new gardening tools.

The woman in question tapped Alice and pointed to her eggs. "Eat."

Their mother looked like his sisters. Petite, blonde, blue-eyed. A stern, sun-wrinkled face, but with a kind smile.

His father, who had yet to say a word, simply watched on with a soft expression on his weathered face.

Once they all finished, the two youngest stood to clear the table.

"Do you really have to leave?" Alice whined, taking Joe's glass. "You've only been here for one night!"

He ruffled her hair. "I do. I must get back. I have a few stops to make before heading home."

His mother sauntered around to him to give him a hug. "You sure you're making the right choice?"

"I am, Mum. Promise."

"I trust you, just want to be sure." She swatted his hair as she headed to the kitchen. "I still expect to come see this flat of yours."

"And I want to see Irene again," Alice exclaimed.

"Yes!" Eleanor cleared some more dishes. "I hope she still wants me to teach her how to curl her hair."

"I want her to visit!" Alice jumped onto Joe's lap. "I want to show her my bugs and the rotting wood!"

Heather stood from the table as well. "If Rupert asks me to marry him, then you'll have to bring her to the wedding."

Eleanor giggled. "Oh, I bet she'd be a real laugh at a wedding!"

Joe gave his littlest sister a hug. "I promise we will come visit if the winter doesn't get too bad."

"Hopefully you don't look as awful then," her other sister laughed.

Alice poked the bandage around his hand. "Did you really punch someone 'cause they were hurting Irene?"

"I certainly did," Joe said, removing his sister and standing.

"Did Irene punch anyone? Has she broken any bones?"

Their mother stood behind the young girl, raised eyebrow and smirk on her face waiting for the answer.

"Irene has punched people, yes. But she knows how to do it without breaking her fingers."

"She's so wicked!"

Their mother clapped her hands. "Alright, Alice, leave your brother alone and get to your chores."

The three of them groaned.

Alice looked at Joe again. "Does Irene have to do chores?"

"Of course."

"And I bet she doesn't winge about it," Mother said.

Joe laughed. "Oh, she does, but she gets them done."

Alice stuck out her tongue, then giggled and scrambled off when Joe gave her a faux stern look.

* * * * *

His father drove him to the train station. They stood by the tracks, waiting for boarding to start.

"I know your mother asked you this. But you sure you know what you're doing?"

Joe laughed. "No, not at all. But everything is pulling me to this decision and I feel like I shouldn't fight it anymore."

The man lifted his son's bandaged hand. "And this new life of yours is worth this?"

Joe's hand hurt, the pain medication made him loopy and his whole body was stiff and sore, but he'd do it all again in a heartbeat if it kept Irene from danger.

"Yes, all of it."

"Can't argue with that."

The train's boarding whistle sounded and the men shook hands.

"I'll ring you later and I promise we'll come visit."

"Take care, son."

Joe boarded the train with a newfound sense of purpose and settled in for the journey back to London.

* * * * *

As soon Joe was back in London, he went to Sarah's street. He had the taxi drop him at the end, so he could walk for a few minutes in the fresh air.

He hesitated before stepping up to her door, but knew he had to. He had put this decision off for months. He knocked and after a minute, his girlfriend answered the door.

"Joe!" She embraced him. "What a surprise! Come in!"

He stepped in and she gave him a once over. "You don't look very good and— Oh my goodness! Your hand! Let me put the kettle on."

Sarah hurried away and guilt ate at Joe like maggots. That imagery, mixed with the pain medication, churned his stomach. This would not be a fun conversation, but it was necessary. Sarah deserved someone who would treat her a lot better than he did – or ever could.

They sat in the living room and the woman looked him over once more.

"Are you going to tell me what happened?"

He went to brush it off, like usual. Or spare her the details of the incident. But then he reconsidered. He was always hiding things from Sarah. Perhaps if he was truthful, then she'd be a little more agreeable to what he was about to propose.

"Irene and I were on a case. We were trapped in a manor. I thought this man had harmed her, so I went after him."

"Bad enough to break your hand?"

He nodded. "I didn't even hesitate."

"So, you punched him?"

"I… He's dead now."

Sarah leaned away from him as if looking at a stranger.

"But that's not why I'm here," Joe said, trying to focus. The sooner he said his piece, the sooner he could let her move on. "I, um… You are… I…I don't think we should see each other anymore."

He clenched his jaw, his insides flipping like flapjacks.

She tensed at his words and sat straight, fixing the hem of her dress. "See each other? I thought we were more than seeing each other. It's been a year and a half, Joe."

"I know. You are so amazing, and lovely, and so kind. But—"

"But I'm not her."

"Who?"

"Irene."

Joe sighed, fidgeting with his bandage. "That's not it."

"It is." She shifted away from him. "Irene as a whole. That flat on Baker Street. Whatever it is you do with your investigating."

He couldn't correct her or argue. She was right; it was everything about his other life that he truly loved.

"I suppose it is."

Sarah kept playing with the hem of her dress, tugging at a loose thread. "There's lots of room for you in my world, but there is no room for me in yours. And you're not willing to budge on your life and make this work, are you?"

Joe looked at the ground. Being truthful to her was both difficult and relieving. While he never lied to hurt her, he was always shifting the narrative or omitting things to spare Sarah's feelings.

The young woman was silent for a long time before she finally stood and folded her arms, cheeks red with anger.

"I knew from the moment I met you that you loved her. But foolishly, I hoped that because she didn't feel that way back, you might turn those feelings toward me. Or you might see that was a life what wouldn't work if we were together."

Joe stood as well, trying to soothe her. "I promise nothing happened between me and Irene. I don't know how I feel about her...."

She let out a light bark of laughter, tears in her eyes. "Then you are a bigger fool than you realise. I only wish you'd figured it out sooner."

"Sarah..." He reached out, but she pulled away.

"You can leave now. I'm pulling a page from Irene's book. Go live whatever life it is you want."

"I am sorry—"

"Just go."

He didn't try to argue or say anything more. There was nothing more to say. He left Sarah's house with some cracks in his heart. He didn't realise leaving her would hurt this much. There was a part of him that felt free, but another was truly sad. He did like Sarah, and had circumstances been different, he would've asked her to marry him within a few months.

But apparently life had other plans for him.

She would be okay. She was beautiful, smart, funny. She would find a husband in no time.

And he would do whatever it was he was meant to do.

* * * * *

Joe ended up walking for nearly half an hour before getting a taxi to the vet practice. Three patients sat in the lobby: two cats and an older lady with a little black Scottish Terrier.

"Hello Dr. Watson!" The Scottie's owner, Mrs. Fields, greeted him. "Oh my, look at the state of you. Had a tussle with a horse?"

"Something like that." He chuckled and crouched to the dog. "Ears still bothering her?"

"Not at all! We're here for her final check-up!"

"That's grand to hear." He gave the dog one final pat, then headed to the examination rooms at the back of the practice. Michael and his assistant were working on a large shepherd, who perked up upon seeing Joe.

"Watson," Michael greeted.

The dog squirmed and Joe stepped back. "I can wait."

"Nonsense. We had to give him something to calm down. Talk to me as he relaxes."

The assistant stepped away to give them privacy.

Joe sat on the floor with the dog and Michael.

"First," his friend said, "you look like hell."

Joe nodded. "Had a bit of a fight during a case."

"Did you win?"

"Yes."

"Good man. Now, what's on your mind?"

Joe hesitated. Speaking to Michael was almost more difficult than his conversation with Sarah. He knew the man would understand his situation and would support him, but he still didn't know where to start.

"I am leaving the practice. I'll finish off the month's appointments and help over Christmas. But in the new year, I'm going to be full time with Irene and the private investigation business."

He kept his eyes on the shepherd as it grew sleepy.

Michael grabbed some tools and sat down next to him again. "Are you as good an investigator as you are a vet?"

Joe laughed. "I honestly don't know. I hope so, or else I'm sure Irene would've chucked me to the curb."

"Can't say I'm surprised." Michael handed some gauze to Joe to wipe the dogs drool. "I was waiting for it all year if I'm honest with you."

Joe looked at his friend. "I love it here, truly. Before the war, I thought it was my calling, as silly as that sounds. But I suppose things changed. I will miss working with you, but you can always call me for tricky cases. And I'll help you find a replacement."

"Don't you worry about that. As long as I can call you if someone brings me a parrot and you aren't off gallivanting in Yorkshire or somewhere."

Joe held the dozy shepherd's head, its tongue lolling out. Gripping the muzzle, he opened the dog's jaw, holding the tongue to the side so Michael could see in.

"Just as I thought," the man said. "Roof of the mouth is all cut up. I bet it's those sticks we told her not to give him. Take a look."

Joe turned the dog's head and sure enough, the hard pallet was nicked a dozen times. There were also a few chips in the dog's teeth.

"Ah, it's the butcher bones."

Michael peered in again and cussed. "How many times do we have to tell her that his teeth are too soft for those? Maybe I'll write a script for absolutely no bones."

Joe let go of the dog, its head bobbing up and down. As Michael chatted, he stroked its soft fur as the dozy dog leaned on him.

Doubt crept in. Was this the best choice for him and his future? If he stayed at the practice, it guaranteed steady income, animals all day and clientele he loved.

No getting shot at. No broken bones. No bad guys.

And yet, he knew he had to leave.

The assistant, back in the room, took over and Joe followed Michael into the office.

"I'll be in on Monday. I can't do much until this hand heals, but I'll see you then."

Michael shook his good hand, then pulled him in for a hug. Joe winced, his body screaming in pain. His friend released him and went to his next appointment.

Joe dug his pain medication from his bag and took two pills for good measure. He left out the back door, knowing that if he went through the waiting room, he'd only get stopped to help.

Instead, he wandered down the street, mind settling into all the changes from the day. He passed the pub he'd eaten at with Lestrade only a few days prior, then the jewellery shop where a pair of green earrings caught Irene's eye on that same day.

The same earrings caught his eye now. By this time, the pain medication was going strong, and before Joe could reconsider, he stepped into the store.

A mere five minutes later, the purchase in hand, he hailed a cab back to Baker Street.

* * * * *

He didn't expect 221 to *look* different, but there was a distinct feel to it now. This was his permanent home, one he had no intention of leaving.

Despite Miss Hudson doing most of the cooking, he'd look at getting a proper kitchen put into their flat. Perhaps he'd even look at expanding the third-floor bedroom. There was plenty of room, especially since there was nothing next to it now but a gaping hole in the building next to it. The decrepit bakery beside them still sat in ruins, the for-sale sign worn by time and the elements. He had no idea what the owner was asking for it, but it was a big undertaking to turn it into the bakery it once was. Plus, 221 Baker Street had a reputation, which Joe was sure played into the sale.

Though, if the people who bought this run-down building happened to know the people in 221, or were, perhaps, the same people, would that make a difference? If the owner was offered a hefty sum to sign over the entire thing, he would surely take it.

The pain medication turned his brain faster than a crank and Joe felt himself nod along to his own good idea.

He dug in his bag for a pen and wrote the telephone number on his hand. Sprinting wobbly to the nearest telephone box, he dialled the number.

Whomever bought the space didn't have to turn it into bakery again. It could be anything. A clothes shop. A beauty parlour. Or an office space for a pair of private investigators.

Chapter XIII

The Beginning of Another Legacy

Irene lugged the Christmas decor back out into the sitting room, determined to have this place cheery for the holidays – even if she felt turmoil inside.

She rubbed her chest. She needed a distraction or another case.

The front door opened and slammed shut. Isla erupted into a fury of barks as footsteps thudded quickly up the stairs. Irene bolted to the fireplace and grabbed the poker. She held it out like a sword ready to confront any intruder. The dog stuck her nose in the crook of the closed door and started whining.

"Isla, come!"

The door flung open.

Irene wound up to swing.

Joe stood in the doorway, out of breath, pupils dilated, as if he'd just walked all over London.

Irene let out a frustrated noise and tossed the fire poker down.

"Dammit Joe. What are you doing?" She snapped at him before remembering that he was mad at her.

He didn't look angry anymore, though, just insane.

He looked her up and down as he stepped into the room. Whatever he saw propelled him forward and he crossed the floor in three long strides. Irene stiffened, but he scooped her into a hug, crushing her against him.

Irene was helpless, stuck against the strong figure of her dearest friend as he slowly rocked back and forth. She had no idea how to react; she couldn't hug him back as her arms were trapped. The hug must be hurting him – unless he'd taken more of his pain medication than he should've.

Joe finally released her, but held her shoulders, gentle and firm. His pupils were huge, the pills obviously in full affect. He let out a big sigh, a big grin on his face. He looked relaxed, excited, as if some weight had been lifted from him.

Irene couldn't quite place why, which frustrated her to no end.

He was cross when he left and was now elated. Had he proposed to Sarah without a ring and she said yes regardless?

Irene needed to distract herself lest she go green in truth. So, she looked Joe up and down and did what she does best;

"You've been to visit everyone, I see. Dirt from Sarah's place, hair from some type of shepherd at the vet practice. And…a stone from the red brick building next store. What have you been up to?"

He laughed, the grin firmly planted on his face.

She scowled. "Does the medication render you unable to speak?"

Joe shook his head. "No. Sorry."

She couldn't stand staring at him anymore. She had no idea what was happening and needed to do something. Turning back to her Christmas decor, she started untangling the paper chain.

"I'm not with Sarah anymore."

"Clearly. As you are here in our flat."

"No, Irene. I'm not *with* her. I broke off our relationship."

She managed to untangle the first part of the chain. What was she supposed to say to him? The silly butterflies in her belly flapped around wildly.

"And I am not going back to the vet practice in the new year."

This was a surprise. Joe loved the vet practice. It was his calling, he'd always said. For him to quit both Sarah and the practice must mean he was leaving London. He surely wasn't going to stay here with no job, no wife, and no prospects.

"Going back to your parents, then?"

She'd almost got the chain knot-free. Then she'd get out the wreaths for the doors.

"I'm staying here, Irene. At Baker Street. With you. We're a private investigation *team*. I made that commitment to you a long time ago and I intend to keep it."

She snorted. "Giving up a perfectly good and normal life just to chase criminals. Miss Hudson would tut-tut at you. What a foolish thing to do, Joe Watson."

The paper chain had run out and in order to get the wreaths, she'd have to turn around. She didn't hear Joe sit down or move, which meant he was still standing a few steps away from her.

"I'd rather be a fool here, with you, any day, then settle for a mediocre life somewhere else."

His words stopped her like a train crashing through a station. This was a trick. His medication was too strong. He was just going to stay for the holidays, then rethink the whole situation. Regardless, she had to look at him. She'd never shied away from any sort of confrontation or awkward encounter, and this would be no different.

She turned. "Do you really mean that?"

Joe never took his eyes off her. "Every word."

Irene's heart hammered in her chest. She stood still, arms folded, chin slightly turnt up, challenging him.

"When I heard that gunshot, I worried it may have been you. I saw the feet, and knew the worst had happened…"

"They weren't even my feet! The maid's were a size and a half smaller and her shoes had buckles."

"I know. I was panicked and in a lot of pain." He stepped closer, turning soft and sincere. "When I thought it was you that had been shot, I realised nothing else in my life mattered more than making sure you were okay. Your words in the cellar…"

She stuck up her nose. "I don't remember what I said."

"Bullshit."

"You can't speak to me like that. I am a lady."

He arched a brow. Though his pupils were huge, the blue still shone through.

Irene sighed, finally cracking. He was obviously determined to have a sincere talk. And though she hated discussing what she felt – as it made her feel weak and incapable – perhaps she needed to get some things off her chest.

"Fine. I remember. But that doesn't mean you should change your whole life! You walked away from two very big parts of your future!"

He waved his hands. "To be with the only part I want to be with."

She rolled her eyes, losing the will to be sincere. "Ridiculous."

Was she worth that to him? Did he really believe in her and care for her that much? He must, or else why would he stay? Because she made him feel guilty for leaving?

Joe stepped closer to her. "I don't know what I'd do if I ever lost you, Irene. I don't ever want to be without you again. For the rest of my life."

"You sound like you are proposing to me."

He laughed. "Maybe I am."

Her heart was in her throat and she shifted on her feet.

She casually wiped her palms on her trousers and scooped up the paper chain.

"You are tired and high on medication. Before you lose yourself completely, help me put this chain up."

"I am proposing."

His words – or perhaps the resolve in them – stilled her completely. She didn't want to turn to him, didn't want to find out exactly what that meant. And yet, she couldn't help it. She spun around, ready to deflect and distract and push him over if he'd dropped to one knee.

He was still standing though.

"A business proposal," he said.

She nearly smacked his broken hand.

"Goodness's sake, Joe. What are you talking about?"

"Let's make this business legitimate. Start up an office. Let's get equipment, pull in all our favours with Lestrade, get a separate phone number. We can hire Annette to be our secretary! We'll have two boards and a filing system and a client waiting room."

All Irene could do was stare. He was elated, bouncing on the balls of his feet like a child at Christmas. And his excitement stirred her own.

However, it was much more complicated than that.

Or was it?

Of course it was, or else everyone would have a business.

For the first time she could remember, Irene's head felt too full of information. This incredible update of Joe's life squished its way into every crevice of her brain. She needed time to process what he was saying, what their future would look like.

"You're high right now."

He grabbed the end of the paper chain and flung it around her neck. "Quite. But no less serious about this plan."

He suddenly swayed on his feet and clutched his head.

"And now you are dizzy. Go take a nap. We'll revisit this when you're not up in the clouds."

He nodded, head bobbling, mess of hair flapping about. He bopped her nose gently, then stumbled toward the door and up the stairs.

Irene stood in the middle of the room, chain still wound her neck.

Isla stared after Joe, then decided Irene was more fun and trotted over.

Irene scooped her up, crushing parts of the chain and the dog to her chest. "Hear that, Isla? He isn't leaving. He's staying right here with us!"

She hugged the dog as tears welled in her eyes.

* * * * *

The next morning, Irene had to make toast and tea all by herself as Miss Hudson was still visiting her father.

Joe stumbled into the room, hair sticking up every which way. He mumbled a "good morning" and plunked down on the dining chair.

"Toast?" Irene asked.

"Please."

She served him, then sat to eat her own food.

As they finished, the telephone rang. Joe stood and scooped up the receiver.

"Joe Watson," he said, then his eyebrows shot up. "Oh! Yes, lovely to speak with you too… I can certainly do that. See you then."

"Who was that?"

He bopped her nose, a lopsided grin on his face. "Someone I need to meet shortly. I won't be long."

He left the room as she called after him. "Remember you look quite awful and your hand is broken!"

* * * * *

Joe returned before lunch looking even more exhausted than he had yesterday. He did, however, stop at the deli for some sandwiches. They ate, then started on the rest of the Christmas decor. They chatted about anything and everything: films, books, different types of dirt, the difference between the wild cottontail rabbit and the black and white domestic ones people kept as pets. It was like they were back to normal. They both looked bruised and cut still, but that was all in a day's work.

They had the wreaths up, the paper chain strung from every corner and Father Christmas sitting on the mantle, with various other Christmas bits and bobbles around the flat. Joe found some cinnamon sticks in a bundle from last year and set them about the place. Soon the whole flat smelled like Christmas morning.

By late afternoon, Irene stood on a stool, hanging twine for the Christmas cards. As she hung the first card, Miss Hudson walked through the door.

"Oh pets, this looks wonderful!"

"Thank you, Miss Hudson," Joe said.

"Go on," Irene climbed off the stool. "Tell her your news."

Miss Hudson gasped in anticipation, but let him speak.

"I am staying here," he said. "To which I mean, that I am living here—"

"He ended his relationship with Sarah and quit the vet practice, so he could stay here for the rest of his life," Irene blurted.

Joe was simply speaking too slow for her liking. She wanted to see Miss Hudson's reaction and figure out if the woman had a letter for her or not.

The landlady gasped again and flung her arms around Joe. "Oh, my dear! Oh, I'm sorry things didn't work out, but oh my! You are here now? Forever?"

"If you'll have me."

She smacked his shoulder. "What kind of question is that! You both are to stay here forever. That's an order."

"Yes ma'am," he giggled.

Irene stepped forward.

"Um, Miss Hudson..." She wasn't entirely sure what to ask.

The woman smiled warmly at her, tears in her eyes already. "I do have a letter here for you, Love."

She dug in her purse and produced an envelope. Scrawled across the front, in her father's handwriting, was her name. Irene reached out but hesitated. Miss Hudson met her the rest of the way and set the letter in her hand.

"Why don't I give you some space—"

"No. Stay, please. You and Joe."

Irene kept her eyes on the envelope as if it might evaporate if she looked away. Joe's hand landed on her back and gently led her to the couch. They sat together and Miss Hudson took up Joe's chair.

"I wrote it," Miss Hudson said. "All but the last line and his signature of course. But he narrated every word, and read it twice to make sure I wrote down exactly what he meant."

Irene's hands shook as she opened the envelope. She reached out for Joe and he immediately intertwined his fingers with hers. She read out loud:

Irene,

My dear child. To hear of your adventures brings me the greatest joy I could ever imagine. Miss Hudson has kept me informed, but her words lack the depth and richness of your cases. I must hear more details. What of the lobotomised girls? And the cipher! I wish to hear all about them.

You must come out and meet the bees. You will find them quite fascinating. As for the violin, I do not play much these days, as my hands are exceptionally shaky, though I should love to hear you play.

I am glad you dug out John's automobile. The look on his face if he saw you driving it around London would be worth a million pounds, I'm sure!

I have sent soil samples with Miss Hudson for you to study. You may determine which seeds would be best and send some with her in the spring. I will grow you whichever flower you wish, my dear.

There are so many things I wish to tell you, but they slip from my mind fast these days. Perhaps I will try to record them, as dear old John did. I do miss him, Irene. Just as I miss you.

Come visit me, my dear. And bring along Joe. He seems like a good asset and a great friend. Truly something that you have your own Watson and Lestrade. We like to collect them like the magpie collects her shiny stones.

Until I can see you again, or travel into London, please send more photographs. They bring memories back more so than words. Also, tell Miss Hudson to not be so stingy with the sweets. Convince her they help my mind as well.

Take care over the winter.

I love you, my dear Irene.

Sherlock Holmes, Father

Tears streamed down her face as a spiked ball of emotions clawed at her throat. She read the letter again silently, then one more time for good measure. A sob escaped her and her shoulders shook.

"Oh, Miss Hudson, thank you."

The landlady was crying herself, dabbing her eyes with a handkerchief. She waved the cloth at Irene, unable to speak.

Joe's arm landed gently on her shoulders, causing a new wave of tears.

"He remembers me, Joe. He remembers who I am."

"You're pretty hard to forget, Irene."

She waved the letter at him, everything blurry through her tears. "He signed it. Look."

"You have his handwriting."

She nodded but couldn't say any more. Joe handed her a handkerchief with which she wiped her face and blew her nose.

Miss Hudson stood, finally able to talk. "This calls for tea."

Irene blew her nose again and tossed the dirty tissue on the coffee table. "I've been so stupid to avoid him all these years—"

"No." Joe cut her off and pulled her into him. "We're not going to start that kind of talk. We will plan a visit out there as soon as we can. Meanwhile, you can write all the letters you want. And we'll use that camera we still have to take photographs and send him a photobook."

Irene nodded, still curled up against him. He smelled freshly shaven, and a bit like mint and leather. It was his usual scent, but one that she hadn't really paid attention to. She felt safe in his arms, like nothing could harm her, like they'd be together forever.

Perhaps they would.

But they couldn't go on like this. Especially if she was to write more to her father, and possibly bring him to London. They would need a separate bedroom for him to stay in, which meant she would bunk with Joe. Which meant Joe needed a bigger bedroom. And they would have to get their own kitchen, because perhaps maybe she should learn how to cook some meals.

She also couldn't be the best private investigator in England – and probably the world – if she didn't have a proper office.

It was as Joe said: they had a secretary lined up and many favours they could call in.

They just needed office space. Shouldn't be too hard, right?

She sniffled the last of her tears and wiped her face on Joe's shirt. Taking a deep, renewed breath, she stood and faced him.

"I accept your proposal."

His eyes widened; red crept into his cheek. "I proposed to you?"

"Yes. And I accept. Let's get an office, and boards, and staff."

He stood as well, his pupils slowly returning to normal. "I was quite high when I said that, Irene."

"I have been on drugs many times and had the greatest of ideas. A good one is just that, no matter the state of mind."

Miss Hudson shuffled into the room with a tea tray. Joe took it from her, placing it on the dining table.

"Miss Hudson," Irene declared. "We are starting a business"

"Oh, Heavens, what kind of a business?"

The front door creaked. Irene recognised Eddy's footsteps climbing the stairs. He stepped into the flat a second later.

"Hello! Though I'd pop in—"

"Eddy, we are starting a business."

He scrubbed his long face with his hand, echoing the landlady's words. "What kind of business?"

She scowled at the lot of them. "What kind do you people think? We are going to need everyone's help. Jeannie, Thom, pull them all in. We will call in all our favours. Clear your schedule after Christmas, this is going to take some work."

She pivoted on her heel and marched to her bedroom. A little touch up of her face and she'd be good as new. Then she could have her tea and start figuring out how to rent office space – and a prime location of course.

She tucked the letter on the shelf next to the photo of her, Father, and Uncle John. She stared at his signature, trying to picture him signing the letter. She assumed he still looked the same. Lithe and tall, with his hooked nose and sharp features. But she had no idea.

A soft knock came from her door.

"Yes?"

Joe entered and stood next to her, gazing at the picture and the letter. He put his arm around her.

She sighed. "Perhaps we will get him into the city to see the office. When we find one."

He gave her shoulders a squeeze. "Come with me. I have something to show you. And bring that picture."

She swiped the photograph and followed him out.

"We'll be right back," he announced to Miss Hudson and Eddy.

They both looked to her for an answer, but Irene just shrugged. Joe led her next door to the half-crumbled bakery. Its front door was still intact, as was the entire first floor. The second floor, however, was completely exposed with moss and mould growing into the brick.

A large SOLD sign hung from the door.

Her partner was grinning from ear to ear.

"Why do you look so happy? This means new neighbours."

Joe dug in his pocket and pulled out a key. "Won't be a bother."

"Did you buy this place?!"

He nodded and unlocked the door. "The second story is all boarded up so the elements wouldn't get to the first floor."

Joe swung the door open and they stepped inside. It smelled musty and old and damp, but not completely ruined. The remnants of the bakery were still present. A large waiting area with a few old tables pushed to the side sat in front of an L-shaped counter with broken glass.

"It will take a lot of money," he said. "Most of the funds we've been saving for the past year. But I thought what better place to have an office than right next door. Then, if you need to do some hard thinking, or take a break, you can just pop to our living room."

He strolled around the main area, boots crunching over broken glass and stones. All Irene could do was stare. This really belonged to them? An entire building to host clients?

Tears welled yet again. How could she have *more* within her?

Joe continued to stroll, pointing at different things. "I thought this area could be just the waiting room. Annette could have her desk here and we could even have a kettle on a table set up for clients. Then upstairs could be the consulting rooms, cosy and warm and safe. And our office. We could set it up like Lestrade and Gregory have their shared space. What do you think?"

Irene clutched the picture close to her chest. "It's perfect."

His eyes widened. "Perfect? You've never said anything was perfect before."

"Well, this place is."

He walked to her and gently rubbed her shoulders. "I'm sorry I didn't confer with you first. I was on a double dose of pain medication and I'm sure the man knew that when he sold this place to me."

She chuckled. "I'm surprised, and miffed, that I didn't think of it first. I feel like that's a saying, is it not? Something about not seeing a forest because of the leaves? Or trees? Or is it a tree you can't see?"

Joe laughed and pulled her closer. She let him hold her, as his lips pressed against the top of her head. They stayed like that for a while. The wind whistled through the small holes in the structure, and the sound of traffic rushed by outside.

"Maybe we can bring my father into the office when it's done."

He kissed her head again. "I think that's a brilliant idea."

She wanted to stay against him, as he was so warm and neither one of them had brought a jacket. However, the drugs must've been working through his system again because he released her and wandered around the building. He went on about the renovations and construction, and some decor he'd love to see.

Irene watched her dear friend with a smile on her face. This was the Joe she'd seen only glimpses of in the past year. The man she knew was waiting the whole time to break free. He was confident, calm, affectionate. The butterflies in her stomach loved it.

He'd asked her if she remembered what she said to him in the cellar, and she did. Every word.

She did love him.

She was probably in love with him.

And she had no idea what to do.

So, she'd concentrate on building their business instead.

The more she looked around the space, and listened to Joe throw ideas around, the more her excitement grew.

Their own business.

A space to interview clients professionally. A place to make a name for herself, to show the world how good Irene Holmes was.

Hugging the photograph tighter to her chest, she let a tear fall.

She would show her father the legacy that Sherlock Holmes left. And everything he had taught her.

Irene would see her father again, and he would remember every moment.

The End

Holmes & Co. will return in:

The Conclusion of Holmes & Co.

About the Author

 Allison Osborne lives in Ontario, Canada with her son, their rabbits, and an overwhelming amount of vintage trinkets. When her mind isn't wandering through 1940s England, she's busy dabbling in scriptwriting and other grand adventures.

Connect with Allison:
Instagram: @allisonoauthor
Website: www.aosborneauthor.com

www.ingramcontent.com/pod-product-compliance
Ingram Content Group UK Ltd.
Pitfield, Milton Keynes, MK11 3LW, UK
UKHW021516180925
463047UK00007B/73